Saving Grace

The Amish Lantern Mystery Series
Book 3

By Mary B. Barbee

SAVING GRACE. Copyright © 2021 Mystic Valley Press. All rights reserved.

Editing Team: Molly Misko, Jenny Raith, and Laura Fry

Cover Design: Zahra Hassan

www.marybbarbee.com

For Yoko, whose beauty and grace stands the test of time.

For by grace you have been saved through faith; and that not of yourselves, it is the gift of God;

Ephesians 2:8

Chapter One

---◆○◆---

Rachel leaned against the counter, her arms folded across her chest. Her face turned a light pink. "Jacob, why do you act like this is nothing? It honestly feels like you're just taking your time. You know you have to go talk to the sheriff about what happened last night. Is there a reason why you're dragging your feet?"

Jacob sighed and set his fork down on his plate next to a half-eaten piece of toast and fried egg. He was exhausted, and his head was pounding. "*Ja*, Rachel. I have every intention of going and talking to Sheriff Streen this morning. What does it matter if I wait to finish my breakfast first? You act like the barn is still on fire."

Grace sat next to her father at the table, watching the interaction between her parents. The Schwartz family never argued. She was taught to exhibit patience and respect with each person, especially her family. She flipped her egg over and her stomach followed suit. Last night was terrible, and Grace worried that it may have caused long-term damage to more than just her father's workshop.

Glancing at Grace, Rachel looked back at her husband, her angry stare softening. She sat down at the table on the other side of Jacob across from her daughter and rested her hand on Jacob's arm. "What we went through last night was *baremlich*. Although it is heartbreaking to see all your beautiful work go up into flames, *liebchen*, we must thank *Gotte* for protecting us from the fire. I am so grateful for the running water that our community had installed, but I can't stop thinking, who would've wanted to harm us? We will all sleep much better when the *gut* sheriff finds the person behind all of this."

Jacob placed his hand over his wife's and looked up from his plate, his kind eyes meeting hers. *"Ja. Denki, my lieb.* I think I am still just a little shocked. And I'm worried, of course." He rose from his seat before a tear could escape his eye and turned toward the oak hat stand he had made when he was a teenage boy. The hat stand was the first piece of furniture brought into the house that the community had built for him and Rachel almost 15 years ago. The hat stand was made to look like a tree with thin branches, and Jacob could remember how his mind was filled with thoughts about the family he would have as he carved each detail in the hardwood. To him, the hat stand represented a family tree, full of love and happiness. He proudly placed his hat on a branch each evening when returning home for the night.

"I will go now. The two of you stay put until we find out more. Even though we had almost the whole community here last night, there may be clues in the yard or out by the shop."

Grace spoke quietly as Jacob adjusted his suspenders and fit his wool felt hat on his head. "*Dat*, please dress warm. I think it is going to be chilly today." She looked as if she had more to say, but she fell silent, her brow furrowed.

"*Ja, dochder*, you don't have to worry about your *dat*." He walked over and kissed his daughter on the forehead. "As a matter of fact, you don't have to worry about anything at all," Jacob said as he looked into his daughter's beautiful eyes. Every day she looked more and more like her mother, and he was very proud of the young lady she was becoming. Rachel and Jacob had decided to name their only daughter, Grace, as a way of expressing their thanks and gratitude to *Gotte*. Unlike many of the families in their community, Grace was an only child. Shortly after their marriage, Rachel and Jacob had received the sad news that Rachel faced health complications and would not be able to have a child of her own. However, the couple, and the community, prayed diligently, and by the grace of God, Grace was conceived and born healthy. She was their special miracle baby, and they loved her dearly.

Rachel rose and met Jacob at the door, reaching out to embrace him with a big hug before he walked out onto the porch. "Do you want me to join you?" Rachel asked. Jacob shook his head and turned to walk down the steps, but Rachel reached out and grabbed his arm. "Jacob, the community will build another shop."

"*Ja*, I know. Let's just take things one step at a time," Jacob said over his shoulder as he descended the porch steps and turned toward the back of the house to hitch his horse and buggy. He realized right away that he had indeed forgotten to wear his coat but he didn't want to turn back. He didn't know how much longer he was going to be able to keep his tears contained, and he didn't want his wife and daughter to see him break down. He didn't want them to have to worry about him on top of the fear that they were all feeling. He stuffed his hands into his pockets and tried to ignore the sick feeling that sat in his stomach like a heavy stone at the bottom of a lake.

Jacob needed to get in his buggy and take some time to himself to summon the strength to discuss what happened with the sheriff. Jacob was confident that he knew why it was his shop that was set on fire in the middle of the night. He was sure it was his fault, and he needed to ask *Gotte* for forgiveness first and foremost. Then, he would tell the sheriff. And then, he would tell Rachel.

Chapter Two

———◆◇◆———

B eth pushed the lace curtains aside and opened the living room window. Small, curved wrinkles appeared in the corners of her smile as the fresh scent of early Spring drifted inside her cozy warm home. This was her favorite time of year, and as she leaned out to look, she was excited to see that the snowdrop bulbs she had planted in her front flower beds last Fall had just started to bloom. Their stark white petals hung down like drops of milk dripping off their stems. Beth inhaled a deep breath of fresh air, closed her eyes and said a quick prayer of gratitude for the beauty that surrounded her.

With Spring, specks of color were popping up all over Little Valley. The blue and yellow wildflowers were rising above the tall grass in the rolling fields on the outskirts of town. The flowering trees that lined the streets were blooming and casting brilliant shades of pink and purple that enticed townsfolk and tourists alike to take long walks, with or without an umbrella in hand.

Along with the light freshness that Spring brought to the air, there seemed to also be a sense of renewal and optimism shared among the Amish community in Little Valley. The trials and tribulations that had hovered over the community the past few months were starting to feel like a thing of the past. And with growing popularity, business was booming all over town. The Amish-owned shops along with small craft booths hosted at the weekly Farmers' Market brought the community good fortune, for which everyone was grateful.

Beth and her twin sister Anna spent most of their time together, their houses sitting on the west side of the community on shared property so that they could remain close even after they married and raised families. But, this morning, Beth was spending extra time alone with her husband, Noah.

Noah, a carpenter by trade and an elder in the community, coordinated building projects for the community.

Since he had returned from helping extinguish the fire at the Schwartz home in the early hours of the morning, he was distracted. Jacob Schwartz had converted his barn into a wood shop for creating and storing his beautifully handcrafted bed frames, dressers and hutches. The flames from the previous night destroyed everything. Beth knew Noah would go to great lengths to arrange for a very special barn-raising event for Jacob and his family.

"*Denki*, dear wife," Noah said as Beth placed a plate of freshly baked biscuits on the table next to Noah's favorite cheesy breakfast casserole. "This looks and smells delicious."

Beth nodded and sat down next to him, reaching for the serving spoon and piling his plate high. Steam rose above the plate, and she warned him it was still very hot as she set the porcelain plate back on the table in front of him. Noah reached for the coffeepot and poured his wife a cup of coffee, topping his off as well. The couple held hands and said the same prayer of thanks that they had muttered each and every day since they were married nearly forty years ago.

After a few bites, Beth started the conversation. She had been so eager to hear all the details of the night before, but she knew Noah was tired from only a few hours' sleep. She practiced great restraint to wait until now to finally dig for information. Living as a high-functioning autistic, Beth had learned a few tricks over the years to distract herself when she was feeling anxious. Saying prayers of gratitude and counting her blessings were most effective, and those were the tricks that had kept her focused this morning.

"I'm so glad no one was hurt last night," Beth said, hoping Noah would open up more about what happened.

"*Ja*, although Jacob's shop is completely burned to the ground, it is a blessing that his family and horse and buggy were all safe." Noah took another bite, "Mmmm, this is so delicious, Beth. I think it gets better and better every time you bake it." He smiled at her, his eyes glinting.

Beth rolled her eyes and smiled back. "You say that every time I cook this casserole, Noah. It is the exact same recipe every time. But *denki*. I'm glad you like it."

Wanting to turn the conversation back to the fire, Beth asked, "Do they have any idea how the fire started?"

"No, not that I know of, but before everyone left, there was talk that someone must have set the fire. With all of Jacob's furniture stored in there, and him being so careful with all of it, I honestly think there's no way it could've happened any other way." Noah shook his head. "But we've had such a nice quiet few months... I hope there is a simple explanation."

"Me, too," said Beth, but she had a familiar sinking feeling in her stomach. "Anna and I will definitely bake something for the Schwartz family and visit Rachel this afternoon. Let me know how we can help with planning a barn-raising, as well."

"Oh, I will definitely lean on you to help plan it. I am heading into town this morning to talk to Moses about ordering the wood and supplies that we will need. Once I have all of that in place, we will get the word out and plan the project. We don't want to waste any time. I'm sure Jacob has a lot of rebuilding that he will have to do to fill orders now that his entire back stock is gone." Noah set his fork down next to his empty plate and leaned back in his chair.

Beth stood to clear the table. Noah asked her, "What else do you have going on today?"

"Well, let's see. Anna and I are caught up with prep for this weekend's Farmers' Market, so there isn't any more baking needed for that. We can even dip into that supply to share with the Schwartz family, I'm thinking. I am meeting both Jonah and Abigail for lunch at the diner - I'm so excited to see them both!" Beth's oldest daughter, Abigail, was ten years older than her youngest son, Jonah. The two siblings always had such a tight bond when they were children, and Beth's heart was warmed watching their relationship evolve as they grew, and their lives changed. Visiting with the two of them together would surely be the highlight of Beth's day.

Returning to her mental list of tasks for that day, Beth continued, "Oh, and I need to get Abigail's old room ready for Eva since she is arriving soon." Beth was looking forward to hosting Eva, especially since she hadn't seen her since she was little. Marianna was Beth and Anna's favorite cousin when they were young girls, and Eva was Marianna's second daughter. Marianna had moved to be closer to her in-laws in Missouri, but she and the sisters exchanged letters often. Recently, Marianna had sent a letter to Beth and Anna asking if Eva could come stay with one of them. Eva was ambitious and wanted to learn a few advanced baking techniques and open a bakery in Little Valley. She had never been married, but she was independent and wanted to establish a business of her own. That sort of autonomy was becoming more and more prevalent among modern Amish communities, and Beth admired her courage.

Noah rarely questioned anything Beth wanted to do, and this was no exception. "A busy day then. That's *gut*. I wish I could join you for lunch, but please tell Abigail and Jonah hello for me. Let's plan to have Jonah over for a family dinner soon. Ever since he moved out on his own,

I feel like I hardly see him outside of worship services. I still don't know why he was in such a rush and didn't stay home until he was more settled."

"Well, he wanted his independence, I guess," said Beth, leaning against the counter. "It's the same with Eva. Kids are different these days. They're more independent and anxious to grow up. The little bit of labor on the farms that he is doing with Eli and Nathan Mast is doing well for him for now, but you're right, he needs to commit to learning a trade because I believe he is terribly unhappy."

"I always wanted him to join me in the carpentry business," Noah said as he placed his hat on his head.

"Right. I know, dear." Beth paused. She knew it disappointed Noah that Jonah didn't want to follow in his father's footsteps. "There's still time for him to follow that path. Let's just keep praying for him to find his way."

"*Ja*, you're right. A great deal of what we see depends on what we're looking for. I should go. I will see you later, dear." Noah hugged his wife and headed out the back door.

Once the breakfast dishes were cleaned and returned to the cupboards, Beth walked into the bathroom to finish getting ready for the day. She brushed her teeth, removed the covering veil from the top of her head, and re-pinned her hair under a freshly cleaned prayer *kapp*. Back in the kitchen, she ran her hands down the front of her pastel pink dress and straightened her white apron before slipping on her shoes. She said one more quiet prayer of gratitude and closed the back door behind her as she stepped out onto the wraparound porch of her home.

Beth turned to see Anna walking briskly towards her, wearing an almost identical dress, *kapp* and shoes. "*Gute Mariye, Schwester!*" Anna called out to her sister.

"I was just headed your way, *Schwester!*" Beth said, returning the warm greeting.

"Oh *gut*. I wanted to check in on you and especially Noah. How is he? Is everyone okay out at the Schwartz's?" Anna's husband, Eli, was already out working the fields this morning, and she hadn't had a chance to connect with him about the fire.

"Come on in," Beth said. "There isn't much I can tell you just yet, but I have a feeling there's more to come."

Chapter Three

Sheriff Mark Streen hung up his cowboy hat as he entered the office. The new hat stand was a gift from the Amish community only recently, and he already enjoyed the little touch it added to the room. The handcrafted detail that Jacob Schwartz took the time to add to each of his pieces was remarkable, and this gift was no different.

Today was an important day for the sheriff. His new deputy was due to report to his first day on the job in about an hour. Sheriff Streen had made a mistake in appointing his last deputy, but he was optimistic that he had made a better choice the second time around. Christopher Jones appeared to be an honest, likable family man with nearly a decade of experience under his belt. His extended family was located just about 45 miles east of Little Valley, and he and his wife were excited to move closer and to feel settled in such a beautiful small town. They had two small boys, not quite school age yet, and Christopher expressed that it was the perfect time to find a new place such as Little Valley to call home. Mark admired Christopher's family values. He hoped that one day he could also share his life with a wonderful wife and one or two children, but he had not crossed paths with the right person just yet.

Most importantly, Mark and Christopher's personalities had a strong natural synergy that Mark was confident would benefit their working relationship and most likely turn into a strong friendship, as well. They were both laid back in nature, easy to talk to and easy to trust. Mark felt that, much like himself, Christopher would approach the law and the people they served with respect. And he was glad to hear that Christopher also enjoyed spending his down time outdoors. In a perfect world, they would together be dedicated to catching criminals, and when things were slow and calm, they could focus on catching some fish.

The front office soon filled with the scent of coffee from the four-cup coffee maker in the nearby tiny kitchen.

Previously a small house, the sheriff's office was renovated about twenty years before, fashioned with one simple holding cell that sat empty most of the time. The office was on the outskirts of town with a couple dozen acres of undeveloped land positioned all around it giving the impression of isolation, even though it was only a few miles down the highway to the Amish community in one direction and a few miles up the highway in the other direction to a few small subdivisions.

Just five minutes before the hour, Sheriff Streen watched Deputy Christopher Jones park on the gravel parking area in front of the office and step out of his car. He was a tall, slender man with a slight athleticism to his build. He also wore a cowboy hat and boots, but that wasn't uncommon among the townsfolk in these parts who weren't from the Amish community.

Before Christopher could reach for the door handle, Mark swung the front door open and reached out his hand. "Good morning! It's great to see you!"

Christopher responded with a firm handshake and a broad smile. "It's great to be here, Sheriff. Thanks again for this opportunity. I'm looking forward to working with you."

"I've been looking forward to this, as well, Deputy," the sheriff said. "Come on in. I'll give you the grand tour of the place." The conversation between the two men was comfortable and easy as the sheriff invited Christopher to hang his hat and then proceeded to show him around the kitchen, bathroom and cell. He pointed to the new deputy's desk which sat to the left of the front door. "I know it's a bit smaller than my desk, and honestly, the desks were here when I moved in. It doesn't make much sense to me for the desks to be different sizes, so I've reached out to Jacob Schwartz to build a couple matching ones for us. He is the fine gentleman who built that nice hat stand right there. He does beautiful work, as you can see, so I'm excited to see how the desks turn out."

Mark's voice trailed off as he was distracted by the sound of a horse and buggy approaching. He looked out the window and said, "Well, that's odd. That's Jacob right there."

Christopher said, "Oh good! I'm excited to meet him."

Mark opened the door as Jacob ascended the steps to the front porch of the office. "Jacob Schwartz! It's good to see you! Your ears must be burning. I was literally just telling the new deputy here about our new desks. Come on in and meet him."

"Good morning," said Jacob. Mark could tell right away that something was wrong. It was clear that Jacob wasn't there to talk about the new desks.

"Jacob Schwartz, meet Deputy Christopher Jones," Mark motioned towards Christopher who approached with hand outstretched.

"It's a pleasure to meet you, Mr. Schwartz," said Christopher.

"*Ja*, nice to meet you, Deputy," Jacob replied.

Mark wanted to jump right into business, so he invited Jacob to have a seat and then asked, "Jacob, what brings you here? Something tells me you're not here to take more measurements."

"No, I'm afraid I'm here to report a crime," Jacob responded, his hands clasped tightly in his lap. He looked at the sheriff, his eyes were red and Mark noted that he looked exhausted. He nodded and Jacob continued, "My wood shop, er, my barn, caught on fire in the middle of the night last night. At first, I wondered if it was something I did, if I was reckless or careless leaving a lantern lit or something, but I just couldn't think of how. The men in our community came together, and we were able to put the fire out, with the help of the county fire department, of course, but not before the whole thing burned down to the ground." He paused and rubbed the back of his neck. Mark thought Jacob might be fighting tears, but he couldn't be sure.

"I'm so sorry, Jacob. I know you must have been heartbroken to see all your work go up in flames like that. I hope no one was hurt?" Mark sat in the old chair behind his desk and motioned for Christopher to pull up a chair next to him. He picked up a large yellow pad of paper and pen and handed it to Christopher.

Jacob continued, "No, sir, thank *Gotte* no one was hurt. But, it is a terrible thing that happened. Like I said, I thought maybe it had been my fault - although I couldn't figure out how - and then I found this note tacked onto the front door of my home." He handed Mark the note.

Holding the note in his hand, Mark read the writing aloud, "'What is your saving grace now?' Hmmm... that's an odd thing to write, for sure. What do you make of it, Jacob?" It was detective work 101 to ask the victim of a crime how they interpreted a clue such as this, and he was happy to see Christopher lean forward in anticipation of the answer.

Jacob sighed. "To be honest, Sheriff, I'm not sure. You know that my only daughter is named Grace, so if the note is referring to her, I am terrified that it means she is in danger somehow. On the other hand, I was thinking that it could just be a reference to my faith. In my religion, the saving grace is a blessing from God that is granted to save a sinner." He dropped his chin toward his chest and looked down at his hands.

"Well, it certainly does sound like the fire wasn't an accident, and this is definitely a clue that can help lead us to the perpetrator," Mark said. After a quick breath, he asked the most important question, "Do you have any idea who would want to burn down your barn, Jacob?"

Jacob shifted in his chair a bit, his eyes still downcast. He answered reluctantly, "*Ja*, I do think I know who did this to me and my family." He paused and raised his face to look directly at Mark, his eyes becoming moist and turning gray as if he were about to reveal a terrible secret. "There is something no one in my community knows. It is something that I am terribly ashamed to admit. To even say out loud." A tear rolled down Jacob's cheek and landed on his crisp white shirt leaving a small dingy wet spot. He reached up and wiped away the tear stain on his face with his sleeve. "About six months ago or so, I ventured into the Little Valley Pub out of curiosity. I had overheard a few men in the community talk about how much fun they had there - even though it is against our rules. I couldn't stop thinking about it. I'm sure it was the devil's work that led me in the doors and sat me down at that gaming table. At the time, it felt exhilarating. I am so ashamed to tell you that, but it's the truth." Jacob shook his head, disappointed in himself, but he continued telling his story, "Well, at first, I was winning a lot of money, and I was having a lot of fun. So then the owner of the establishment, Sam Graber, invited me back, and I was flattered, in a weird way. I went back a few times. Secretly, you understand. And before I knew it, I was hooked. I felt like I had gotten the hang of the game, plus I had built trust with the owner so much so that he offered for me to play with money I didn't even have. The winnings could be even bigger that way. I don't even know why I cared about the money. In my community, we don't strive to be rich with material possessions. But, you see, it got messy and things got out of control."

Mark sighed and leaned back in his chair. His stomach turned somersaults. *I knew Samuel was up to no good!* he thought to himself. He had only recently shut down the gaming tables at Samuel Graber's bar on the instinct that the games were not being regulated legally, and it turns out his instincts were right. Letting players get in over their heads, playing with money they didn't have, was certainly far from legal... or ethical, for that matter. There was no place for that in Little Valley.

The sheriff snapped out of his thoughts as Jacob continued with his confession. "I ended up losing more money than I had. And I ended up owing Mr. Graber a lot of money." Jacob wiped away another tear. "I didn't have the money, and I couldn't figure out how to pay him back without revealing my secret to everyone." His breathing quickened, "That's when Samuel showed up at my house. Thank *Gotte* that my wife and daughter weren't home that day. He demanded the money, but I still didn't have it. He threatened to hurt me if I didn't pay him, and I promised I would find a way to pay it the next week."

Mark knew where this story was going, but he remained silent to let Jacob continue with his story uninterrupted.

"Then, I went to the bar with some of the balance owed, hoping to buy more time. I had to pull from my family's savings. Mr. Graber was sitting alone with Mr. Davis, the owner of the new bed-and-breakfast in town. Mr. Graber said that they had been talking, and he didn't want my money - which was a relief at first - but he wanted to call it even if I could convince the men in my community to sell him the extra lots of land we own. You see, when we first established our community here in Little Valley over twenty-five years ago, the community all pitched in together to buy extra lots of land. We wanted to make sure we had plenty of room to grow. And we have definitely grown and built on some of those lots over the years, but there is still quite a bit of space that is undeveloped. Mr. Graber said that he and Mr. Davis want to build some sort of park for recreational vehicles or something like that, and they want our land for that."

Jacob stopped and inhaled a long deep breath. "Sheriff, he just wouldn't take no for an answer. I left there with the money I brought, but with a much bigger problem. I tossed and turned for the next few nights. There was no easy way for me to convince the community to sell that property, especially when Mr. Davis had already been harassing us about lowering our prices at the market and in our stores. Everyone thinks he is trying to take control of the market and push us out of business and maybe even out of Little Valley."

The sheriff nodded. Christopher was taking notes quietly next to him, his eyes on the notepad.

"So, I summoned the courage to approach him again. It was just a few days ago. I tried to explain to him that our land would not be for sale, but that I had every intention of paying him back the money I owed him." Jacob wrung his hands and shifted in his seat again. "Mr. Graber became furious, and he told me I had exactly one week to find a way to sell him our land. Or I would regret it. He was very unreasonable, but I didn't think it would go this far. Now I don't know what to do. He won't let me pay him back, and the land is not mine to sell." Jacob's eyes widened as he leaned forward. "I'm not afraid to admit that I am scared,

Sheriff. I'm scared for my family and for my community. I don't know how to stop him from hurting me and the ones I care about."

Mark wished he could make this right, but unfortunately, an anonymous note and no other clues did not warrant an arrest of Sam Graber. And the illegal gaming practices in which Jacob participated made things even murkier with the law.

"First of all, thank you for your honesty, Jacob. I can't advise you on the ethics of lying or how to approach this in your community, and unfortunately, considering the entire situation, I can't even honestly provide you with much protection. However," the sheriff said slowly, "I *can* promise to move swiftly with an investigation into the cause of the fire. The best-case scenario is we find a clue on the scene that leads us to arrest Sam Graber for arson. So, go home. Make sure no one even walks around that burned barn of yours. I need to call the fire department first, but we'll head that way right after I hang up the phone."

Jacob stood, thanked the two men, and headed swiftly out the door.

Mark picked up the phone and dialed the number to the Mainstay County Fire Department. "Hi, yes, this is Mark Streen, Mainstay County Sheriff. I'm calling to talk to the chief about a fire in Little Valley that occurred last night or early this morning."

As he sat on hold, waiting to speak to the fire chief, he looked over at Christopher. "If you want a cup of coffee, you'd better grab it now and drink it fast. It looks like it might be a pretty exciting first day on the job for you."

Chapter Four

T he sheriff's car drove up slowly and parked in the gravel driveway just to the side of the Schwartz home. Sheriff Mark Streen and Deputy Christopher Jones stepped out on either side of the car and tipped their hats almost simultaneously to greet young Grace who was sitting on the porch swing. The swing was painted a deep red, a perfect contrast to the steel gray color of the Schwartz home.

"Is your father home, Grace?" Mark called out. He knew Grace from a previous case solved just months earlier, and he was impressed by her manners, intelligence and confidence, especially for a young teenage girl.

"Yes, sir. He's right around back. Feel free to walk on back there. He's expecting you." Grace answered before rising to her feet to head back inside.

"Thank you kindly, Grace," the sheriff responded with a smile and another quick touch to the brim of his hat. The two men took only a few steps around the side of the house before they had a full view of the charred remains of Jacob's workshop. Hanging in the air was a faint smell of smoke mixed with the pungent odor of wet burned wood. The men found Jacob behind his house, just as Grace directed. He was lying on his back on the ground, his head and shoulders hidden under his Amish buggy. The men could see a nearby small handmade stall, made just big enough to hold the one horse comfortably. It was cozy and practical, well built and sturdy. The horse inside the stall whinnied quietly and shook its head almost as if it wanted to communicate with Jacob that someone had approached.

"Hey there, Jacob," the sheriff called out. Jacob jerked as if the sheriff had startled him. It did not surprise Mark that he had been lost in his thoughts after all he had confessed in the sheriff's station that morning. Jacob dropped the wrench he had in his hand and scrambled to his feet, brushing the dirt off the backsides of his trousers.

"Sheriff. Deputy." Jacob greeted each of them with a quick handshake. "Thank you for coming out. I've tried to keep everyone away from the, uh, shop, like you asked. But, we had almost all the men in the community here last night, so I'll honestly be surprised if you'll find anything clue worthy."

"Right. It's a long shot, for sure, but we'll take a look, all the same." All three men stood facing the crime scene. There was a moment of silence before Mark spoke again. "No need for you to follow us, Jacob. Christopher and I will go check it out and let you know if we find anything."

Jacob nodded, and the sheriff and deputy headed towards where the barn once stood, stepping carefully, eyes focused on the ground in front of them. There were dozens of footprints in the wet mud left behind after the men had sprayed water to extinguish the fire. The many footprints could have been from the work boots of the community or the firefighters, some from smooth-soled boots similar to what Jacob wore that day, as well as a few different types of general sneakers. There was nothing distinctive, and most of them were footprints on top of footprints. Mark and Christopher agreed that, unfortunately, the prints wouldn't be of any help.

Not finding any clues at first glance in or around the charred ashes either, Christopher suggested they split up and look a few yards out in all directions on the dry land to see if they might find any signs of anyone who had approached the barn that evening. After a thorough search, the two men came up empty-handed. The only tire tracks they found were from the fire truck and tracks from buggy tires.

Mark had learned a good deal about the Amish community since he had arrived in town less than a year before, and he thought it was unlikely that any of them would be responsible for the fire. It disappointed him that the search turned out to be fruitless. The only evidence they had was the note Jacob had found tacked on his door. The question, "What is your saving grace now?" was confusing. After what the town had just recently been through a few months ago, Mark truly hoped that this note wasn't a threat for sweet Grace Schwartz. The best-case scenario was that it was a simple poke at the Amish faith, meant to scare Jacob enough to get results.

The sheriff and deputy returned to Jacob's backyard and found him leaning against his house sitting on a perfectly wrapped bale of hay. His eyes were closed. His hand rested on the top of the hat next to him. The gentle breeze blew a few strands of his hair in and out of his face ever so slightly. As the two men approached, Jacob opened his eyes and stood on his feet, quickly placing his hat back on his head.

Trying to hide his disappointment, Mark reached over to give Jacob's shoulder a firm pat and said, "Well, sir, we didn't find any clues or anything helpful out there, but we've still got the note. The deputy and I will take a harder look at that and we'll do some digging around town. We'll get to the bottom of it. You just stay safe and take care of your family. Let me know if you think of anything else, of course." The sheriff leaned in and with his voice lowered, he muttered, "And stay away from Sam Graber, Jacob. Even if you offered to give him what he asked for, it would never be enough. He would just try to take more. Promise me you'll stay away from him and keep your nose clean. If he did this, we'll find out and we'll book him."

Jacob nodded as his shoulders slumped forward. "Thank you, Sheriff. Thank you both for your time," he responded. It was evident to both Mark and Christopher that Jacob had hoped to sound strong and confident, but his voice was thick with worry.

Just as they turned to leave, Noah Troyer approached from the side of the house. "Good morning, folks," Noah said. He nodded to Jacob and patted him on the back and reached out with a welcoming handshake to Mark first, and then to Christopher. "Not sure we've met," he said to the deputy.

"Mr. Troyer, this is Christopher Jones, the new deputy of Mainstay County," Mark introduced him proudly.

"Pleasure, sir," Christopher greeted Noah with a warm smile and a firm handshake.

"Please, call me Noah. It's a pleasure to meet you, as well," Noah said. Turning to look back at Jacob, he said, "I guess we all know why you two are here. It's terrible what happened to Jacob's shop and all his beautiful furniture. I hope you were able to find something to help find out who did this to him."

"Unfortunately, we weren't able to uncover any more information, but we're going to do our best to find out who the culprit is, for sure," Mark said. "We want you all to know that we are here to protect you. Please don't hesitate to reach out if you need anything at all." Christopher nodded in agreement.

"Thank you, sir," said Noah. "Jacob is a good man, and we've already got plans in motion to help him rebuild."

"You've got a great community here, men. It's really incredible to see how much you care for one another," Mark responded. "Well, we've got a case to solve, so we'd better get busy. Have a good day, and like we said, Jacob, we'll be in touch with any news."

The sheriff and deputy returned to their car and slowly pulled out of the gravel driveway, headed back to the office. "It sure was great to meet Noah. He seems like a good guy," Christopher said.

Mark turned on his blinker to make a right turn onto the highway. "Oh yeah, just wait until you meet his wife and her twin sister. Those two are quite the pair, and something tells me you'll probably meet them sooner rather than later."

Chapter Five

------◄◊►------

"What a great idea to meet for lunch today, *Maem*!" Abigail was the spitting image of her mother. She had the same kind blue eyes, straight nose and welcoming smile that the twins shared. She sat across from Beth in the front window booth of Little Valley's diner. The view from the window included the local coffee shop, her son-in-law's hardware store, and Matthew Beiler's flower shop, all lined up in a neat row across Main Street.

"Your *dat* and I were just saying this morning how we don't get to see enough of you children. Everyone's lives seem so busy all the time," Beth said, lifting the silver pot of coffee to pour herself a cup. Steam rose into the air just below her face as she stirred one blue packet of sugar into her drink.

"Well, *Dat* does always say, 'Blessed are they who are too busy to worry in the daytime and too tired to worry at night," Abigail grinned.

Beth chuckled, "*Ja*, that is true. That is one of his favorite proverbs, for sure." Turning the conversation a bit more serious, she continued, "Unfortunately, he is living quite the opposite today. I guess you heard about the fire at Jacob Schwartz's home last night?"

"*Ja*, it is *baremlich*. Jeremiah joined the men to help, but he was of the last to hear and arrived just as the fire was extinguished. He said it burned the entire barn to the ground. There was nothing left." Abigail's husband, Jeremiah, worked as a leather smith, creating and selling custom horse saddles to his customers. Earlier that morning, Jeremiah described the heartbreaking scene to his wife, his own eyes brimming with tears as he imagined the heartbreak of Jacob seeing all his hard work burst into flames.

Abigail adjusted her posture to sit up straighter and continued, "I'm glad that my *bruder* isn't here yet, actually, because I wanted to talk to you about something in private."

Beth placed her coffee cup down on the table and met her daughter's eyes, with one brow raised slightly higher than the other. She felt a pit in her stomach again, and she immediately knew that it wasn't good news she was about to hear.

Abigail cleared her throat. "I'm just going to get right to the point." She took a deep breath and then the next words came rushing out as she exhaled, "Jeremiah and I are thinking about leaving Little Valley." She dropped her gaze down to the table and traced the line that the sunlight was casting on the dull surface with her finger. She didn't need to look at her *maem* to know that this news would upset her.

Beth gasped dramatically and placed her hand over her heart. "What?! No! You can't leave, *Dochder* - I won't let you!"

Abigail raised her eyes to meet her mother's. "*Maem*. You know I'm not a child. The bottom line is that Jeremiah and I are worried about all the crime in Little Valley. It doesn't feel safe here anymore. We love being close to you and *dat*, and the rest of the family, but we have to protect our children... your grandchildren." Abigail was referring to her beautiful twin boys and their younger sister, but she also wanted to have more children and Jeremiah was hesitant to continue growing their family in a town surrounded by danger. The recent murders had originated the thoughts of the move, but then last night's fire had pushed more urgency into her husband's voice when they discussed it further that morning.

Abigail reached out to hold Beth's hand. Her mother's skin felt paper thin and the age spots seemed more apparent today than before as she struggled with the thoughts of moving out of town. Glancing back up at her mother's face, she immediately saw the tears welling up behind the blinking eyelashes.

It was Beth's turn to clear her throat. She swallowed back the tears and responded, "This is your home, Abby. What would it be like for all of us if you and Jeremiah and the kids were not at the worship services? Where would you go? Jeremiah would have to start his business all over again." She paused and squeezed her daughter's hand before pleading, "Tell me you'll pray about it long before you make such a big decision."

"Of course, *Maem*, of course. Jeremiah is not the type to make rash decisions. We are only discussing the possibility now, and we are not telling anyone. As a matter of fact, he would probably be upset with me if he knew I told you. He wouldn't want you to worry. And neither do I." Abigail knew her mother well enough to expect her to run to her twin sister, Aunt Anna, and figure out a way to convince them to stay - and maybe that's why she'd told her. Abigail didn't want to leave, but she also knew that Jeremiah's arguments and concerns were valid.

Just at that moment, the two women were greeted by Abigail's favorite *bruder*, Jonah. "*Hallo! Wie bischt, Maem and Schwester?*" He leaned over and embraced Beth with a warm hug, changing her mood immediately, before sliding into the booth next to Abigail and throwing his arms around her neck.

"Where'd you come from, *bruder*?" said Abigail, teasingly.

"I know, I'm late," Jonah grinned. He quickly pushed back the blond curl that had fallen in his eyes. "I've had a busy workday already, and it's only now lunchtime."

Beth's face beamed. Jonah's presence had pushed her sadness to the back of her mind. "You look so *gute*, my *sohn*. I bet you are *hungerich*."

Abigail jumped in, "Jonah is always *hungerich*, *Maem*. Have you forgotten already?" The three laughed heartily. Abigail was so relieved to change the subject, and she was delighted to see her little brother again. Ever since they were young, the two had gotten along famously. When he was a toddler, Jonah always chose to sit in Abigail's lap. And as he grew a little older, Abigail helped Jonah with his studies and read to him at bedtime. It was hard to move out of the home when she was married, but she welcomed Uncle Jonah into her own children's lives, and they loved him just as much as she did.

Abigail was very proud of the young man Jonah was becoming, but since he had returned from *Rumspringa* and moved out of her mother's home, she rarely saw him. She felt as if there was so much to find out about his life, and she knew her mother felt the same way.

"*Ja*, let's eat!" Jonah said, rubbing his hands together.

Noticing that Jonah had arrived and giving them a few minutes to read the menu, Jessica, the owner of the diner, approached the table a few minutes later. She was wearing a beautiful broad smile and her eyes twinkled. "Are y'all ready to order?" She asked, her notepad and pencil in hand.

"I think so," Beth answered for all of them. "Go ahead, Abigail," she nudged.

As Abigail began to recite her order, the bell on the front door rang and Matthew Beiler entered. Jessica looked up as he came in, and their eyes met. Holding up a manicured finger, she politely interrupted, "Excuse me, one second, please."

Jessica called out, "Welcome to Heaven's Diner! Please have a seat, and I'll be right with you."

Matthew responded with a wave and the same big smile, his eyebrows raised ever so slightly. "Take your time, Ms. Jessica," he responded, as he took a seat.

Jessica reached up and flipped her hair back off her right shoulder, and Abigail couldn't help but notice that her cheeks had turned a light shade of pink. Abigail and Beth exchanged glances and grinned as they watched the scene unfold. It didn't take a wise woman to see that there was something a little extra happening in the exchange between those two.

Then, noticing Beth, Abigail and Jonah at the table, Matthew called out, "Ah, *gut daag*, Troyer Family!"

The three responded with warm welcomes and pleasantries.

Jessica paused to allow for conversation between the two tables. After a brief moment, she returned her focus to collecting their orders and cheerfully asked, "Ok, so where were we?"

Chapter Six

A bigail reached over and picked up the coffee pot on the table. Jessica had just refreshed it before heading off to prepare the table's lunch order. Jonah leaned forward to sniff the aroma of freshly brewed coffee beans as Abigail filled his cup. She topped off her mother's cup next, and then her own.

"So, little *bruder*, tell us how you've been," she prompted.

Jonah took a long sip and set his cup back down on the table, already half-empty. He relaxed against the back of the tall booth seat cushion. "I've been *gut*. I've been *gut*," he said. "There's a lot of work to be done between Uncle Eli's farm and Mr. Mast's farm. Those two are definitely keeping me busy."

Beth interjected, "Are you learning a lot?"

"*Ja*," Jonah answered flatly.

Beth pushed a little bit further. "Do you enjoy the work?"

"I guess so," Jonah said. "As much as you can enjoy work, I guess."

Beth sighed and responded, "Well, Jonah, you know that no dream comes true until..."

Jonah chimed in and they finished the sentence in unison. "...you wake up and go to work," they said.

Jonah shook his head. "I know, *Maem*, I know. You sound like *Dat.*"

Abigail sat quietly. She knew Jonah was going through a phase of wanting his independence. So many Amish boys learn their father's trade and grow up to follow in his footsteps, but for whatever reason, Jonah was resisting that path for himself.

"I don't want to be a carpenter, *Maem*. I know that I am letting you and *Dat* down, but I need to figure out my own way in life. I don't want it handed to me. And honestly, I'm not as talented at woodwork as *Dat* and Mr. Schwartz are. Nor do I enjoy it as much." Jonah sat up and leaned forward resting his elbows on the table. "I get bored easily with that stuff, *Maem,* making the same furniture all the time, using the same tools every day. It's not that I'm lazy. I want work that has more variety, I think."

Beth nodded, and both took a sip from their coffee cups at the same time.

Abigail asked Jonah, "Do you make good money working on the farms, Jonah?"

"It's not bad," Jonah said, "but since Eli and Mr. Mast are mostly teaching me and didn't necessarily need an extra hand on deck, I feel guilty that I am taking extra from their pockets."

Beth shook her head, "No, Jonah, that's not true. They are happy to have you helping them."

"It is true, *Maem,* but don't worry, I work hard to bring extra money into their businesses. I try to pay my keep, I guess you could say. I still would love to find something that provides a passion for me. I would love to find something of my own." Jonah clasped his hands together, his face turned up briefly "I pray for it every day, and I have faith that *Gotte* will give me what I am looking for in due time."

"*Ja, Gotte* is *gut,*" Beth agreed. "Let your *dat* or I know if you need anything, *sohn.* We both support you in your journey and want you to be happy."

"Ok, *Maem*, *denki*, but I know *dat* is disappointed. He wants me to work with him, I know this." Jonah emptied his cup and leaned back again.

Beth cringed slightly and responded, "Jonah, come to dinner and have a talk with your father. Like you are talking to me and your sister here. He will understand, but you have to explain it to him. Maybe he can even help you find what you're looking for."

"My saving grace," Jonah muttered as Jessica appeared with their food on a rolling cart.

"We have the club sandwich and fries for the wonderful Mrs. Troyer," Jessica said, as she set Beth's plate on the table in front of her. "And we have the broccoli cheese soup and garden salad for you, Sweetie" she recited, setting down the bowl and plate on the table in front of Abigail. "And finally, we have the cheeseburger and fries for you, Young Man," Jessica said as she picked up the last plate off the cart and set it down in front of Jonah. "And we have ice water for everybody. You have napkins on the table there by the window, and ketchup right there, too. Is there anything else I can get y'all?"

Beth spoke, "This looks wonderful as always, Jessica. Thank you so much!"

"You're so welcome! Enjoy!" Jessica sang out as she walked back towards the kitchen. She glanced over at

Matthew's table and called out, "Your lunch is almost ready, too, Matthew." He responded with a smile.

Beth said quietly, "*Händt nunna.*" Abigail and Jonah joined her by placing their hands in their laps, closing their eyes and bowing their heads in silent prayer. Just a minute later, Beth uttered "Amen," and Abigail and Jonah responded "Amen" in unison, lifting their heads and reaching for their silverware.

Abigail changed the subject. "*Maem*, how is Aunt Anna? Is her knee fully healed?" Several months ago, Beth and Anna had gotten into a wreck in their buggy and Anna had to walk with a cane for some time afterwards.

Beth smiled and nodded, "*Ja*, she is back to taking her daily walks and moving around like it was never hurt. She sends her love to both of you today."

"Oh, *gut, gut.* Please send our love back to her." Abigail said between bites of lettuce.

"And I guess you both know that Eva is coming to stay with us for a little while?" Beth asked, holding her sandwich in one hand and a french fry in the other.

Jonah looked up from his meal, "Oh, she is? I didn't know. Is everything ok? Why is she coming to Little Valley?"

Beth swallowed her bite and explained how their cousin was visiting to learn baking skills from Beth and Anna.

"She has dreams to open her own bakery one day. She makes the best fudge I've ever tasted, which is difficult to make... but she wants to learn specifically about baking breads and pies. I am looking forward to having her."

"I will have to come by and see her after she gets settled," said Abigail. "She and I always had so much fun when we were young girls, and I haven't seen her in ages!"

The conversation continued as Beth shared how well things were going at the Farmers' Market, Abigail shared the latest funny stories about her children, and Jonah learned about the fire at the Schwartz home. Rising out of the booth to head back to their busy lives, Abigail noticed Jessica sitting across from Matthew. A half-eaten piece of apple pie and a cup of coffee sat on the table in front of Matthew, and a glass of water in front of Jessica. The two seemed very comfortable, like old friends, laughing and enjoying fun conversation.

Beth raised her hand and called out to Jessica as she, Abigail and Jonah headed for the door, "Thank you, Jessica, for lunch! We'll see you next time. Matthew, have a great day! We'll see you for dinner on Sunday at Anna's, I hope?"

Jessica scrambled to her feet, her cheeks turning pink again, and waved goodbye. "Thank you for coming in," she called out. She headed toward their table to grab the dirty dishes.

Matthew turned toward the door and responded, "*Gut daag! Gut* to see you all! And yes, I'll see you on Sunday, Mrs. Troyer!"

The diner door shut behind them. Abigail turned to Beth and said, "Are they...?" Beth shrugged her shoulders, her eyes wide and eyebrows raised. Jonah chuckled and shook his head, "Nothing gets by you two. Abby, you are becoming more and more like *Maem* every day." Abigail grinned, threw her arms around her mother's shoulders and exclaimed, "Well, that's a compliment!"

Chapter Seven

---◆◇◆---

I t was just past noon, and Hank Davis's stomach was growling. He knew he needed to get back on a better schedule, but it always felt like there was still so much to do to be ready for the Amish Inn grand opening. He jumped up the front porch steps, returning from a quick visit with Wyatt Nichols, the owner of the garage next door to Hank's bed-and-breakfast establishment. With a bribe in hand, Hank had been able to get Wyatt to agree to limit the use of the shop's air compressor to late morning or afternoon hours after the grand opening. When Hank scouted a place to set up a bed-and-breakfast, he didn't think about how loud the garage would be, and he suspected that the noise might become an issue with guests, especially in the early mornings.

The team meeting that Hank had scheduled was set to start in about ten minutes, so Hank headed to the kitchen to grab a quick snack. He passed Peggy Fremont in the living room. Neither said a word to the other. Peggy was busy dusting the antique furniture. Fifteen years in the cleaning business, Peggy was accustomed to being invisible to her house cleaning clients, especially to Hank. She was thin but fit, her mousy brown hair swept up into a high ponytail. Stray strands of hair framed her face. She was a single mother of two young girls and was grateful for the work. Not unlike the rest of the employees working for the Amish Inn, Peggy looked forward to the business that the grand opening would bring.

Hank entered the kitchen and found Ryan Green, her strong hand gripping a wooden spoon, stirring slowly in a big pot. She greeted Hank when he entered, "Hey there, Hank." Ryan was a tall woman with broad shoulders and thick blonde curly hair that would fall just past her shoulders if she didn't have it tied back in a low ponytail just below her chef's cap. She held herself in a way that meant she was not to be messed with. Her voice was firm and confident, her eyes piercing and intense. Even her name evoked masculinity and strength. Hank had never met a woman named Ryan, but her name didn't matter to him since she was meant to be hidden in the kitchen. So far, she seemed to be the right one for the cook's position at the Amish Inn.

Hank's stomach ached when the aroma of the beef stew hits his nostrils. "That smells incredible," Hank responded. "I'm starving. When will it be ready?"

"Oh good. It's ready now. I was thinking about sharing it at the meeting and see what everyone thinks. It's an Amish beef stew, you know. I found the recipe online." Ryan grabbed a ladle and filled a large soup mug with the thick brown stew from the pot.

"I would hope it would be Amish, seeing as that is what I hired you for," Hank snapped. He snatched the mug from her hand and grabbed a spoon from the silverware drawer.

Ryan rolled her eyes. "You have terrible manners, has anyone ever told you that?" She asked the rhetorical question with her hands on her hips.

"Hmmm. Mmmm," Hank responded with a mouth full of really hot beef stew. He opened his mouth and waved his hands in front of it, as if it would cool it down. He rapidly grabbed a drinking glass from the shelf, yanked open the refrigerator, and pulled out the gallon of milk. He poured a bit of milk into the glass and gulped it down, hoping to cool off his mouth. "Aaahhhh," he grunted as he exhaled.

"Serves you right," Ryan said. "Didn't you see me take it straight out of the pot?" She chuckled, and Hank was annoyed.

"This tastes like store-bought stew, not homemade stew. It needs more work. I expect you to serve our customers dinners that blow their minds. This stew isn't it." He set the mug down and grabbed a granola bar from the pantry. "The meeting is starting in a few minutes," he said, and he turned and left the room.

Back in the living room, Hazel Thompson, Logan Clark and Sebastian Lee had joined Peggy. Logan was the maintenance man, or handyman, as Hank referred to him, for the bed-and-breakfast and Sebastian took care of the landscaping and outside building mainte-nance. Logan was a skinny young kid in his early twen-ties with light hair styled in a crewcut. Sebastian was the complete opposite of Logan. Sebastian was a large, burly, older man with long dark hair tied back in a long braid. He wore a black bandana rolled up and tied around his head, covering most of his forehead.

Logan and Sebastian were standing in the back of the room chatting about the most recent baseball game, but their chatter ended once they realized Hank had entered the room.

Hazel was Hank's assistant. She was a petite middle-aged woman with small square glasses placed precariously on her turned-up nose. She was sitting in one of the large upholstered chairs, her laptop open and balanced on her legs.

Peggy was on the couch next to her, looking at her phone. She quickly turned off her phone and slipped it into her back jean pocket when Hank entered the room.

"Find a seat, please, fellas," Hank instructed as he pulled a chair from the window area to sit in front of the others. He hollered out for Ryan to join them, and she appeared in the doorway in a few seconds. She leaned on the doorframe, refusing to take a seat without exactly saying those words.

"Ok, good. We're all here. Let's keep this short. We have a million things to do in the next couple days." Hank gestured to Hazel to take the lead on the meeting's agenda.

Hazel started out by mentioning how the rooms at the Amish Inn were already booked out through the first three weeks. She looked up at Hank for feedback. Hank responded to Hazel with a flat tone, "Good. Please continue."

Moving on, she began to address each item on the list of remaining tasks to be completed, asking for each person to acknowledge their responsibilities and give their assurance that everything would be completed on time. Hank responded when necessary, reminding each person to keep in mind that the inn was to represent the Amish lifestyle in every way possible. He expected everyone to do their part selling the Amish goods he had displayed throughout the bed-and-breakfast, the baked goods that Ryan would be preparing, and even the flowers and plants that would be on display out on the front porch.

"I expect all of you to know a lot about the Amish culture by now, so that you can answer any questions our guests may have. Ideally, we want our guests to experience all of it here, not to go looking for it in the shops in town." Hank paused before continuing. "Ok, I think that's everything. Everyone can go back to work," Hank instructed with a wave of his hand. The Amish Inn team members quickly dispersed and went their own separate ways to tackle each one of their tasks leaving Hank sitting alone in the living room. He let out a sigh of relief. *I think this is going to work*, he thought.

Chapter Eight

The afternoon sun was shining bright over Little Valley, the sky a brilliant blue scattered with puffy clouds that looked like cotton. Anna was lounging on her front porch enjoying the beautiful day while patiently waiting for her sister to return from lunch. Her legs stretched out in front of her, her feet resting on the edge of the patio table as she sat leaning back on the soft cushions covering the wooden porch swing. Beth's husband, Noah, had built Anna's porch swing for her and Eli some time ago as a wedding anniversary gift. It was the perfect anniversary gift because sitting on the swing side by side in the warmer evenings quickly became one of the couple's most treasured ways to spend time together. Like Anna and Eli, the swing was older now, its surface covered in fine lines, but it remained sturdy and comfortable. Every few years, Noah would apply a beautiful dark cherry stain on the aging wood.

Moving back and forth in a slow rhythmic motion, the swing creaked quietly as if it were singing a sweet melody and Anna's thoughts drifted as she closed her eyes.

Little Valley was the only home Anna ever knew. She was so grateful for her family, her friends, and the quaint little town. The land that she and Eli shared with Beth and Noah provided a beautiful space to call home and a bounty of wonderful vegetables and fruit. Eli's farming business earned more than enough income needed to raise their children and save for their future. For this, Anna was especially grateful, but despite their seemingly perfect life on the farm, Anna and Eli had recently discussed what it would take to relocate and convince their family to move somewhere safer. They could not ignore the crimes that had taken place over the last year. There were murders before, and now Jacob and Rachel Schwartz's barn was burned down to the ground. They were again terribly concerned for the safety of the community, and for their family.

Anna had shared her thoughts of leaving Little Valley with her sister several weeks back, to which she wasn't the least surprised when Beth reacted with tears. It was almost as if Beth lived in denial, hiding from the truth, and so much so that she was even able to convince Anna recently that her own thoughts were silly and that it would somehow get better. Anna knew she could never leave her twin sister behind, so she needed to convince her and Noah to consider that it might be time. A long deep breath exhaled Anna's lips. She was sure that would take a lot of prayer.

The clip-clop sound of Beth's horse and buggy brought Anna out of her worrisome thoughts. She opened her eyes and greeted her sister with a big smile, raising her hand in the air to wave at her. Before grabbing her purse and the box of cinnamon rolls that she had packed for the Schwartz family, Anna instinctively checked to tuck any stray hairs into her *kapp* and bounded down the porch steps.

"Well, it took you long enough," said Anna, with a grin on her face. She jumped into the buggy and held on tight to the door handle on her right. Ever since the sisters' buggy had turned over and crashed, Anna felt more comfortable holding on tight.

"*Ach du lieva*, you act like we're going to drive full speed to see Rachel," Beth said with a chuckle. She rolled her eyes and signaled the horse with a kissing sound to trot forward. "What have you been thinking about up there on your favorite porch swing?"

Anna responded, "Nothing. I was just enjoying the freshness of Spring." Beth glanced over at Anna, and Anna was sure that Beth knew she wasn't telling the whole truth. It was almost impossible for the sisters to hide anything from each other.

"*Ja*, it is a gorgeous day," Beth answered.

Changing the subject, Anna asked, "How are Jonah and Abigail doing?"

Beth proceeded to catch Anna up on Abigail's funny stories and Jonah's struggles with Noah. Anna was grateful for the distraction. Beth was still talking when their horse and buggy pulled up in front of the Schwartz home. Rachel was sitting on the top step of her porch designing a beautiful planter with yellow daffodils, blue and yellow primroses and purple and pink violas. She looked up and greeted the sisters with a smile and a wave as they stepped out of the buggy.

"*Gut daag*, Rachel!" Anna called out as they approached, Beth chiming in with the same greeting.

"I see you are welcoming Springtime," Anna said, gesturing toward the flowerpot.

Rachel set her gardening tools down and stood. "*Ja*, I got these flowers at the market last weekend and I'm only just now getting around to planting them. I'm glad I waited though, because it is just what I needed today. I was planting the primroses and thinking about the proverb about being grateful for the roses instead of complaining about the thorns." She cast her eyes down and then looked away. Anna could see that she was fighting tears, so she reached out and gently squeezed her arm for reassurance.

"That is one of my favorite proverbs," Beth said. "We are here to help, Rachel. No one should have to face this kind of thing alone, so please let us know how we can lend a hand."

"*Ja*, and we want to talk to you, too, about the best timing for a barn raising, as well," Anna chimed in.

Rachel removed her gardening gloves and wiped her cheek with the back of her hand. "*Denki*. To both of you. Really. It means the world to me that you are here and helping organize that. Jacob has a lot of work ahead of him to rebuild all the orders he had completed and lost. I'm sure that is overwhelming him. He is at Noah's right now, working with his tools and supplies to try to get a head start. He will have to figure out what he has on his plate and where to start. It will be a huge undertaking since all the details of his orders went up in flames with his work. He and Noah spent most of the past few hours rummaging through the destruction seeing if any of the metal tools... or anything at all... survived the fire."

Rachel suddenly slapped her hand on her thigh and gasped, "Where are my manners? Please do come in. I will put on a pot of coffee... or tea? And we can sit down and catch up before we get down to business."

Chapter Nine

---◆◇◆---

J acob pulled his horse and buggy up to the front of the Packers' house. Before jumping out of the buggy, he bowed his head and said a quick prayer, hands clasped together in his lap. *Gotte, please give me the strength and courage I need to face my failures. I will accept whatever you think is best for my consequences but know that I seek forgiveness with a full heart of sincerity and so much gratitude for this wonderful life you have given me. It is because of you that Rachel and I were blessed with Grace and so much more, and it is my dream to lead a more faithful and honorable life with you by my side.*

Raising his head, he inhaled a full deep breath and stepped down onto the ground. Jacob patted his horse on the head lovingly as he reached for the reins and tied him to the stake set up in front of the porch for visitors like himself. He silently counted the steps on the way up to the front door, hoping to settle his racing heart before he came face to face with Bishop Packer.

When he reached the door, he paused for a moment. The door was made with a few large pieces of walnut lumber, the knots from the tree defined among the different dark shades. Jacob remembered when the bishop had requested he craft a "unique front door" made of this very special wood. Wood such as this was typically used for flooring, not necessarily doors, and Jacob was skeptical of how the finished product would look. But he ended up having a wonderful time creating a unique panel pattern that was simple enough, but with just a touch of something extra special. He was proud to see that it still looked flawless almost twelve years later.

Jacob knocked politely. Margaret Packer opened the door and greeted Jacob, "*Gut daag*, Jacob! It is *gut* to see you. Please come in. Joseph is expecting you. Would you like some tea?"

Jacob nodded his head and returned the greeting, "*Denki. Gut daag*, Mrs. Packer. It is nice to see you, too." He couldn't help but notice that Margaret was quite thin, her face looked tired, and Jacob wondered if she was well. He made a mental note to encourage Rachel to pay her a visit soon.

"No, *denki*, Mrs. Packer, no tea for me this afternoon. I just had a tall glass of water before heading this way," he said.

Jacob followed Margaret into the small room beside the living room. It held a simple wooden desk and matching hard chair. A ficus tree sat in the corner on one side of the room's only window. A tall-back upholstered chair sat on the other side with a small round table to the side and a floor lamp positioned behind it. The bishop was sitting at the desk when Jacob entered. He turned around right away, and rose to his feet, his arm outstretched to welcome him with a handshake and a one-armed hug.

"*Hallo*, Jacob Schwartz. *Wie bischt*?" The bishop smiled at Jacob, a warm smile, his kind eyes twinkled.

Jacob responded with the same warmth, "*Denki* for your time today, Bishop. It is a beautiful day, and I don't want to take much of your time."

"Nonsense," the bishop said, waving his arm in the air. "Have a seat, and please, tell me what's on your mind."

Jacob nodded and sat down in the upholstered chair. He welcomed the comfort of the soft cushion, and he wondered how many men before him must have sat in the same chair with worries to share. Surely, none of them could be as severe as his, he thought, and his heart again began to race. He cleared his throat and his voice cracked slightly as he told the bishop everything. The words came rushing out like rain through a broken gutter, spilling on the ground. It was a bit of a relief to finally sit face-to-face with the bishop and to tell him all of his mistakes and fast held secrets. He looked down at the floor through the entire confession, ashamed to look the bishop in the eyes. The bishop sat silently listening and allowing Jacob to speak without interruption.

"...so, that is why I'm here," Jacob concluded. A tear escaped his eye and trickled down his cheek. For this last sentence, he took a quick breath and summoned the courage to look up and meet the bishop's eyes. "I am so sorry, Bishop Packer, and I am not ashamed to beg for forgiveness." The bishop's head moved only slightly, and Jacob couldn't tell if it was a nod. So, he continued, "Rachel and I are forever grateful for this community. It is our home. Our family. What I did was unspeakable, and to think that I have brought danger to everything - and everyone - I care so much for... well, it breaks my heart. I have asked *Gotte* for forgiveness, too, of course. It would be a blessing if you would give me the chance to make things right. I would do anything."

The bishop held up his hand slowly as to gently interrupt Jacob. His eyes narrowed a bit, and he said softly, "*Denki*, Jacob, for coming to see me today and for sharing this with me. I can see that you have regrets. As you know, we have shunned men in the community who have gambled at the Little Valley Pub in the past, but none of them came to me to bare their soul and ask for forgiveness in this way. It was the right thing to do to first ask *Gotte* for forgiveness. The next step will be to forgive yourself."

Jacob nodded and brushed another tear from his cheek, his eyes locked with the bishop's as he listened intently. "*Ja*, that is most difficult, I agree, Bishop. I also have yet to confess to my wife. She has been through so much, and I do not want her to worry."

Joseph interjected, "Oh, you must do that right away, Jacob. Rachel is a kind woman. You must trust that she will provide you comfort and not judgment in the end, but the sooner you have an honest conversation with her, the better."

Jacob nodded again. He waited to hear of his fate with the community. He took another quick breath and was deciding how to ask if he and his family could stay, but as if the bishop was reading his mind, he continued with his answer.

"As for the community, I will speak with the elders, but I am confident that everyone will agree with my thoughts. You and your family have been a big part of our community here in Little Valley. We do not want to see you leave, especially since you are asking for forgiveness. We will grant you forgiveness but be prepared to inform everyone about what we are facing." The bishop tugged on his beard. "I will stand next to you and provide whatever support you need, but it is the right thing to do."

Jacob nodded. He had already expected this would be necessary. He knew it would be difficult, but he trusted it would be the safest thing in the end.

"We were so sorry to hear of the fire - and so relieved to hear that no one was harmed." The bishop paused for a moment and rubbed his eyes. "We still have a problem, though. It's Sam Graber, and possibly Hank Davis, too. We are going to have to figure out what we need to do to protect our community."

Jacob pleaded, "What can I do, Bishop? I will do anything to make this right, but I am so lost. The sheriff told me to stay away from Sam and Hank, but I'm not sure..."

The bishop interrupted, "Absolutely, do not approach Sam. Let me discuss this with the elders and we will decide on the next steps. You just go and take care of your family, Jacob, and talk to your wife. I'm sure there will be a barn build to help with your losses, and it may be just what we need. Barn builds are always such *wunderbaar* quality time with everyone." The bishop smiled and leaned forward to touch Jacob's arm, lifting gently as Jacob stood. "I will be back in touch with you in the next few days to work out the logistics of the announcement and more. Get some rest. This has taken a toll on you, and you need to take care of yourself." He paused before continuing, "And don't forget what I said about the importance of forgiving yourself." He hugged Jacob and walked him to the front door.

Jacob thanked Bishop Packer again before climbing into his buggy and heading home. His shoulders felt so much lighter, and he was eager to tell his wife next. On the road home, Jacob glanced up at the sky, his right hand covering his heart and he said out loud, "*Denki*, my Lord. You are my saving grace."

Chapter Ten

---◄○►---

Arriving at the Little Valley Pub just minutes before his shift started, Archer Melgren pulled into the back lot and parked next to Sam's truck. Sam Graber was the owner of the pub and Archer's employer. Archer detested Sam and everything about him. His loud, boisterous voice grated on Archer's nerves. Sam's lack of manners and terrible customer service made Archer question how he was even in business. Even the sight of Sam's large bright yellow truck with black trim evoked an unsettling feeling.

Archer shifted his Toyota Camry into park and wrapped up his phone conversation with his mother. "I'll call you tomorrow, Mom. I just pulled up to work," he said, reaching to grab his phone from the mount on his dashboard. "I love you. Have a great day today!"

He slipped his phone into his pocket and grabbed the keys out of the ignition. A defeated sigh escaped his lips before he opened the back door of the pub and entered the dimly lit storage area. It's only a means to an end, he reminded himself. Archer had big dreams of going to law school, but he had made some poor financial decisions during his first years of college and found himself overwhelmed with debt from a failed business venture he had fallen into with some close friends. The debt would need to be resolved in order to obtain funding to further his education.

Archer's Uncle Jack lived in Little Valley and had invited Archer to move in with him temporarily until he could get caught up with things. Jack Melgren was a regular customer at the Little Valley Pub and had become acquaintances with Sam Graber. Any chance he could, Jack reminded Archer how he pulled some strings to get him the bartender position. Archer was grateful for the income but working for Sam was far from pleasant.

Turning around to lock the back door behind him, the sound of Sam's boisterous voice traveling across the otherwise silent pub greeted Archer like an icy gust of wind on a cold day.

"Archer, is that you?" Sam hollered from his seat at the front bar.

"Yep!" Archer responded, attempting to set a positive mood with his tone. "It's me." He walked into the front area and behind the bar. Sam and Hank Davis were sitting at the bar. Sam had a short glass of what Archer knew to be whiskey, Sam's drink of choice. It looked like Hank was only nursing a glass of iced water.

"Hey there," Archer greeted them. "How's it going this morning?" He began to unload the clean glasses from the dishwasher, placing them carefully on the shelves behind the bar.

"Morning, Archer," Hank responded with only a second of eye contact. Sam grunted as he finished off his drink. He set the glass down, tapping it on the bar and motioned for Archer to pour him another.

Archer could quickly tell that he had interrupted their conversation, so he poured Sam's drink and turned his back, slicing lemons, limes and celery on the counter at the back wall.

"I'm no idiot, Sam. I know you hate them," Hank said.

Sam responded, cool as a cucumber, "You *are* an idiot if you think I am the one that set their barn on fire. Yeah, I'm not a big fan, but if I wanted to hurt them, I wouldn't have set *a barn* on fire. I think maybe you don't know me like you think you do." He chuckled.

Archer felt his shoulders tense.

"Look, all I'm saying is that I want nothin' to do with that foolery," Hank continued. "You know the Amish Inn is opening in just a few days, and I don't want any trouble from them... or from the law."

Sam scoffed, "Yeah, good luck with that. The law is one hundred percent on their side, all the time. If you're a suspect in that fire, then you're gonna have trouble."

"That's my point," Hank responded, running his hand through his hair. "I don't wanna risk everything I've put into this. I know we tried to bully that guy, Schwartz, into lettin' us have their land. I don't want nothin' to do with that now. If anything, I need those people to trust me right now, and burning down their barns ain't gonna help with that. Just leave them alone, Sam. If something happens and I get blamed, I can't promise I'll have your back."

Archer heard the movement of a bar stool pushed across the hard floor. He turned to see Sam standing over Hank, his face leaned in close, his eyebrows drawn together and his finger pointing just an inch from Hank's face. "I said I didn't have nothin' to do with that fire, Hank. You try to turn over on me, and I'll make sure that you regret that you ever knew me. I've done a lot for you and that stupid Amish Inn idea of yours. I can destroy it just as fast."

Hank stood and puffed out his chest. "I'm not scared of you, Sam. And I'm not comin' for you either. I'm just saying, let it go. Messin' with them is a losing battle. It's only going to lead to more trouble for you and the pub. As much as you've done for me, I've done for you." Hank turned to grab his keys off the bar and winked sarcastically at Sam, responding, "Keep your threats in your pocket. They don't work on me."

Sam's face relaxed a bit, and he took a small step back before resting again on the bar stool. "Yeah, yeah. Mr. Tough Guy. Go back to your little Amish hotel. I got nothin' else to say to you."

"Yeah, that's a first," Hank chuckled as he walked towards the front door.

Sam turned his attention to Archer. "What are you looking at?" He asked before tipping his glass back again.

"Just pulling inventory," Archer replied, hoping that his voice didn't give away any discomfort he was feeling.

"Yeah, well make sure you get it right this time. The next time we run out of Jack Daniels, the lost sales will be comin' out of your pay." Sam stood and walked back to his office leaving his empty glass on the bar. A moment later, Archer could hear the door slam.

Chapter Eleven

B eth and Anna headed back to the parking lot where their buggy was parked to retrieve the remaining storage bins of cookies, leaving Eli and Noah to finish setting up their table and banner. The air was crisp, and the sky was overcast, filled with light gray clouds that threatened rain.

"I hope we don't get rained out today," Beth said, pulling her shawl tighter.

"*Ja*, me too. I overheard someone say that the rain is predicted to hold off until this afternoon," Anna responded, tucking away stray strands of hair that had slipped out from under her *kapp*.

"Is Eli sticking around with us this morning?" Beth asked.

"*Ja*," said Anna, thinking back to her and Eli's conversation over breakfast just hours earlier. Eli confessed he had mentioned their thoughts about moving out of town to Noah. Anna wondered if Noah had said anything to Beth yet. She never kept secrets from Beth, and it felt terribly uncomfortable to do so now. But she justified it in her mind that it was just a conversation between Eli and herself. There were no plans in place. They only spoke about possibly traveling to visit some nearby communities to see if they were safer and a good fit for a future home, but they had not committed to a date or anything of that nature.

"You seem distracted, *Schwester*. Is everything ok?" Beth asked, reaching into the buggy and handing one of the containers to her sister. She grabbed the other bin and the two women headed back.

"Everything is fine," Anna responded, slowing down her pace.

Beth slowed her pace to match her sister's. "Something is on your mind. I can tell," she insisted.

"*Ja*, I have a lot on my mind lately, but everything is fine. We should sit down and have a cup of tea after the market this afternoon. I feel like you and I haven't had a chance to connect in a few days." Anna looked at Beth. She hoped she wasn't causing her stress. She knew that she had a lot going on in her life with Eva's arrival scheduled for the next week and with a bit of friction between Noah and Jonah. Beth was a worrier and Anna had always felt like she needed to protect Beth, not add to her worries.

Beth nodded and smiled. "I would love that. I was just thinking the same thing this morning. Plus, we need to put the plans together for the Schwartz barn raising. That's right around the corner."

Beth and Anna returned to their booth just as Eli and Noah were setting up the chairs and cashbox. Their table looked beautiful as always with a colorful patchwork tablecloth that Beth and Anna had sewn together several years ago. The tablecloth had turned out just as they had imagined, representative of an Amish handmade quilt. Each square displayed a unique handmade pattern, mostly pictures of hearts, lanterns, horses, and flowers.

On top of the tablecloth sat a stainless-steel tiered display of cookies on one side and the clear plastic case of pastries on the other. Three pies with spatulas next to each sat in the center of the table. The apple pie had apple shapes cut-out of the top crust, the sugar cream pie had a golden meringue top layer, and the dark chocolate pie had a contrast of white dots of whipped cream placed uniformly around the outside rounded edge. Boxed orders ready for pickup sat organized and labeled below the table on a small bookshelf that Noah had created when their business began to grow, and pre-orders had come into play.

A simple banner reading Amish Baked Goods stood at the back of the booth. The sisters had not particularly wanted to display a banner, but it was required in the vendor rules for the market. The two women had agreed upon a pale blue background with a white basic font for the design and had ordered the banner and its stand from the Little Valley Print Shop. It was not an inexpensive purchase, so they made sure to take extra care of it, storing it in its original tube each week.

"This looks great, as always, fellas! Thank you so much for your help!" Beth said cheerfully.

Eli nodded, and Noah responded, "Glad to help. Good luck today, ladies. I think you're all set here. I'm going to head over to Jacob's booth to give him a hand. Eli, you're staying though, right? I will be back later to help with the breakdown."

"Sounds *gut*," Eli responded. "Good luck with Jacob's booth today, too. I know he appreciates your help."

"*Denki, lieb,*" said Beth. "Have a *gut mariye*. I'll see you later today."

Anna was already helping their first customer when Noah headed towards the parking lot. Beth jumped in to help the next customer, an English woman with her young child in a stroller.

"My husband and I just love your cinnamon rolls," she said. "We have made it a tradition to have them every Sunday morning," she laughed and then she leaned in and placed one hand flat next to her mouth as if she was sharing a secret with Beth and Anna. "I'm not gonna lie, your goodies are so much better than what they have at the bakery in town. Everyone knows it, too." The woman winked at Beth.

Beth and Anna looked at each other. Anna knew instantly that Beth was uncomfortable with the customer's comment, so she stepped in and replied, "Thank you so much. I'm glad to hear that you and your husband enjoy our cinnamon rolls! They are a crowd favorite, for sure." She collected the woman's money and responded, "See you next week!"

After the woman packed the box of cinnamon rolls in the netting at the bottom of the stroller, she thanked the sisters and walked on to continue shopping.

Anna checked in with Beth. "Are you ok?" She muttered under her breath, with a smile still set on her face for customers walking by to see.

"*Ja*, I'm fine. You know those sorts of comments make me cringe," Beth said. Her eyes were downcast as she adjusted the displayed goods so that they were all the same distance from each other on the table in front of her. Anna knew that organizing and "making things perfect" was a coping mechanism for Beth's autism, so she took a step back from the table and let Beth continue sorting things on the table and in her mind.

Anna took a moment to survey the crowd. There were so many unfamiliar faces. Anna could remember when the farmers' market customers used to be all the same people. Now, people drove in from neighboring towns and counties to visit Little Valley. Their farmers' market had become well-known, and word had begun to spread. Watching all the people greet each other used to be Anna's favorite part of selling at the market, but the crowd's energy was different now.

I wonder if the person who started the Schwartz barn fire is here today, Anna thought to herself.

"Well, good morning, ladies!" Shannon Graber stood on the other side of the table, a broad smile spread across her face. "And, Mr. Miller," she nodded to Eli who sat in one of the chairs near the back of the booth. "How is everyone doing this fine morning?"

"Hi there, Mrs. Graber!" Anna responded.

Beth chimed in, "Welcome, Mrs. Graber!"

"Oh please, you know you can call me Shannon," Mrs. Graber insisted. "How's business? I feel like I haven't seen you in a while."

"Yes, we were thinking the same thing. You haven't been here in a few weeks, it seems. Is everything ok?" Anna asked. Shannon Graber was a regular customer at the sisters' market booth, and the women were always glad to see each other. She was so kind and always complimentary. For several years, she purchased their baked goods for every event she had, from weekly Bible study nights to an occasional baby shower. Anna and Beth really enjoyed seeing Shannon each week, and it was a shock to find out that she was Sam Graber's mother.

"Oh yes, everything is good. I have been out-of-town visiting my sister the past couple of weeks." Shannon looked to her left and then to her right and said, "Beth and Anna, I am so sorry to hear about the fire. Sam was just telling me about that yesterday when he came over for dinner. I hope no one was hurt."

Beth jumped in and said curtly, "It's a blessing that no one was hurt, but the whole community is pretty shook up about the whole thing."

"Yes, it was indeed terrible," Anna interrupted Beth before she could continue. Word had spread through the community that Sam Graber was behind the fire, but she was sure that Shannon had nothing to do with any of it. And Anna didn't want Beth to come across as rude or accusatory. "We are relieved that no one was hurt, and we are coming together to build another barn for the Schwartz family soon."

"I am so glad to hear that," Shannon continued, her eyes soft. "I have always been so impressed with how your community cooperates to support each other. I know it has been a rough few months for all of you, and I am not alone when I say that Little Valley is here to help if you need anything." She paused briefly and then continued, "And I hope that the horrible person who set the fire is caught and punished very soon. I can't imagine what the motive could've been to do something like that to such nice people like y'all."

"Well, thank you, Shannon," said Anna. Then, wanting to change the subject, she asked, "Have you tried our new dark chocolate pie yet? It's pretty popular."

Beth agreed, "Yes, we worked hard to perfect the recipe, and the feedback we are getting is that it is just wonderful."

Shannon was convinced. "Oh! Well, I must take a piece for myself for tonight then, and is there any chance I can order a batch of your sugar cookies for Wednesday night's Bible study?"

"Absolutely!" Anna said. "We can deliver those to you early next week and you can pop them in your refrigerator until Wednesday."

"Perfect!" Shannon responded. She collected her nicely wrapped piece of pie after handing the payment over to Beth. "Thank you so much. It was great to see you! I'll see you in just a few days then." She wished Anna, Beth and Eli a good day and headed off to continue her shopping.

Just as Shannon walked away, Jessica McLean walked up to the sisters' table. She was cheerful as always. "Good morning!" Jessica said, dragging the words out as if she were singing a song.

The sisters greeted Jessica by returning warm smiles and hellos. Beth bent down and pulled two boxes out from below the table.

"We have your orders right here," Beth said cheerily.

"I knew you would," Jessica responded, grinning. "My customers at the diner are starting to expect weekend butterscotch cinnamon rolls. You two can never stop baking these," she winked.

Anna replied, "Of course not. We also included a new strawberry cream cheese danish for you to try. We haven't started selling them yet, but we will be harvesting fresh strawberries soon enough and we wanted to have something a little different to offer this year."

"Oh, yum!" Jessica clasped her hands together in front of her. "That sounds delicious! Anytime you two need someone to test your recipes, I'm in!"

Olivia Black appeared out of nowhere and stood next to Jessica. "What's this about a strawberry cream cheese danish?" she asked, looking over her glasses at Anna.

Anna saw Beth clench her hand into a fist out of the corner of her eye. Olivia Black owned the only bakery in Little Valley. The shop's catchy name was Something Sweet. The first few times the sisters had met Olivia, they didn't know she owned the bakery. She presented herself as a customer, buying one of everything, before Jessica told Anna and Beth who she was. She had been purchasing their goods to judge her competition. Olivia had even approached Jessica recently and asked her to stop selling Beth and Anna's baked goods in her diner. Olivia offered Jessica a deep discount to purchase and sell the desserts from Something Sweet instead, but Jessica declined. She knew her customers looked forward to Anna and Beth's delicious treats, and she wanted to support their business.

"Hi, Olivia," Jessica said, without the same melodic tone as her earlier greeting to Beth and Anna.

Olivia ignored her and began inspecting what was in the plastic case in front of her.

"Good morning, Mrs. Black. Can I help you find anything today?" Anna asked politely.

Olivia had long gray hair that extended past her shoulders, pulled back away from her temples with small clips. Small metal framed glasses were perched near the end of her small pointy nose, and crow's feet surrounded her dark eyes. "What do you have that's new?" She asked, pushing her chin down to again look over her glasses at Anna.

"Well, our dark chocolate pie is probably our newest item today, but you tried a piece of that last week, if I remember right." Anna responded with a small smile.

Beth interjected, "Yes, how did you like the chocolate pie, Mrs. Black?"

Olivia ignored Beth and continued, "What are the strawberry cream cheese danishes I heard you talking about? When are those coming out?" She asked, sounding annoyed.

Anna didn't like the way Olivia ignored Beth, so she turned to Beth to allow her to answer Olivia's question instead. Beth took the cue and responded, "Oh, we are still just working out the kinks in the recipe for those. We don't have any for sale just yet."

Olivia shifted her attention to Beth. "I see," she said, squinting her eyes as if she were suspicious of Beth's answer. Without another word, she turned on her heel and walked away.

"Wow. I'm sorry she is so rude to you," Jessica said. "You two don't deserve that. It must be hard to be kind to her when she is so disrespectful."

Anna waved her hand as if to brush it off. "No worries, Jessica. *You* certainly don't have to apologize for *her* behavior. It doesn't bother us. "

Beth chimed in, "We have a proverb that says, 'Kindness, when given away, keeps coming back.' It's not always easy to remember that, though, I'll admit."

"Well, if that's true, then your lives should just be overflowing with kindness! I always say that it makes perfect sense that two such sweet women like you would bake the most delicious treats. You are definitely in the right business," Jessica smiled and thanked Anna and Beth one more time before gathering her order and heading off to open the diner for breakfast.

"She is such a nice girl," Anna said, watching Jessica walk away.

"Oh, I agree," said Beth, leaning her hip on the table. "And something tells me Matthew Beiler feels the same way."

"What? What do you mean?" Anna asked, her curiosity piqued.

"I guess I didn't tell you that I saw them at the diner together when I was there with Abigail and Jonah? The two definitely seemed to be happy to see each other." Beth grinned sheepishly.

Anna rolled her eyes. "I really like Jessica, but I can't imagine Matthew wanting to date an *Englisher*."

Beth raised her eyebrows and closed her lips together. "You're probably right," she said, but she didn't believe it. She was confident that there was some chemistry between those two, but Jessica wasn't Amish and Matthew had just been baptized weeks before since returning to the community.

There's no denying that a relationship between those two could become problematic, especially considering the current growing friction in Little Valley between the Amish and the English. The only way it would work is if either Jessica joined the faith or Matthew chose to leave the community. She made a mental note to include Matthew and Jessica in her evening prayers. She was hoping for the first option.

Chapter Twelve

"Mmmm, mmmm," Sheriff Mark Streen said as he pushed his gear shift into park in front of the home of Amish elders, Solomon Fletcher and his wife, Charity. "I can't believe this happened again," he muttered as he pushed the driver's door open and stepped out of the car. The smell of burnt wet wood hit their noses, an odor too familiar to both the sheriff and the deputy.

The Fletcher home was right next door to the Schwartz's property, separated only by about an acre of trees. The Fletcher family was highly respected in the Amish community. Their family was one of the first families to settle on the land in Little Valley, and this second arson meant that the sheriff and the deputy would have their hands full convincing the rest of the folks that they were safe.

Sheriff Streen mounted the porch steps, skipping every other one, and Deputy Jones was right behind him. Isaac Fletcher, the Fletchers' oldest son, greeted them at the door. Isaac invited the two men into the home, after a brief introduction, to find Solomon sitting on a rocking chair in the living room, his walker parked within his reach next to him. Solomon's wife, Charity, was sitting on the couch. Both Solomon and Charity were frail. Mark guessed that they might be in their late eighties.

"*Maem, Dat*, have you met Sheriff Mark Streen? And this is the new Deputy, Christopher Jones." Isaac gave an introduction as if he knew the two gentlemen; however, they had only just met a minute before at the front door.

Both men removed their hats and nodded a hello to Charity to which she responded with a small smile. The sheriff reached his hand out to Mr. Fletcher, bending over at the waist. Mr. Fletcher reached out and shook the men's hand, one after the other, first shaking Mark's hand and then the deputy's hand right after, remaining seated. "I hope you don't mind if I don't stand," Mr. Fletcher stated. His accent was thick, and he spoke each word slowly and carefully.

"Not at all," Sheriff Streen responded with a wave of his hand. "We won't keep you long," he continued. "We were so sorry to hear about last night's fire, sir. Did any of you see anything?"

"No, nothing. But get him the note, *sohn*," Mr. Fletcher said.

Isaac stepped into the dining area to retrieve a note from the table and handed it to the sheriff. Mark immediately recognized the same type of heavier paper as the note that Jacob handed him just the week before. He unfolded it and found the same neat print with black ink. At first glance, it looked like the same handwriting, and he looked forward to comparing the notes side-by-side. This time, the note read, "Got any more aces up your sleeve?" Mark suppressed a sigh. This brought even more direct suspicion to Sam Graber, considering the gambling reference. He needed more than inferences, though.

Christopher pulled a smaller plastic evidence bag out of his back pocket and held it open for his partner. Mark dropped the note in the bag without a word and turned back to the Fletchers. "Pardon me, ma'am," he nodded to Charity and turned his focus to Solomon and Isaac who was now standing right behind his father. "Do you have any idea who would want to set fire to your barn?"

Isaac rested his hand on his father's shoulder and responded, "We all know who is behind these fires. It's Samuel Graber. Jacob confessed everything to the community on Sunday after service, and the note explains it all. Please, Sheriff, can you arrest him now?" Mark recognized the frustration in his voice.

"Unfortunately, we need more evidence," Mark said, "but we are going to do everything we can to put an end to this. I promise." With these last two words, he held his hat to his heart and looked directly at Solomon. "If it's okay with you, the deputy and I will take a look around the crime scene, er, your barn. And then we'll get out of your hair."

Solomon nodded, and the two men followed Isaac to the back door. Standing on the back porch, they could see what was left of the barn. It looked as if the Mainstay County Fire Department arrived a bit earlier this time, leaving a shell of what used to be the barn instead of just a pile of ashes like at the Schwartz's property. Starting their search, Mark and Christopher were disappointed to find the same dozens of footprints layered on top of each other, the same fire truck tracks mixed with those of horses and buggy wheels. There was nothing left behind in the rubble that they could see. Mark feared that it would be another dead end.

The two men returned to thank the Fletcher's for their time and give more assurances that they would put a stop to the terrible crimes happening against their community. They jumped back in their car and pulled out of the driveway. Instead of heading back toward the highway, Mark turned on his blinker to turn left. He didn't have to explain it to Christopher. The deputy knew where they were headed.

Chapter Thirteen

---◆◇◆---

S am Graber was standing outside, leaning against
the wall, smoking a cigarette when the sheriff's car
pulled into the parking lot of Little Valley Pub. Sheriff
Mark Streen made eye contact with Sam as he stepped
out of his vehicle.

"Just the person I was looking for, "the sheriff called
out. Sam didn't respond. Instead, he took another drag
on his cigarette and paused a minute to size up Deputy
Jones with his eyes.

"Well, lookie here, you must be the new deputy dog," Sam said with a sarcastic grin, his words dripping with disrespect.

The deputy planted his feet, straightened his shoulders, puffed his chest out just a bit and stuck his thumbs in his belt. He set his eyes with a cold hard stare directed right back at Sam and slightly cocked his head. He didn't say a word.

Sheriff Streen spoke to Sam again, breaking up the staring match that Sam and Christopher seemed to be having. "Where were you last night around one in the morning, Sam?" The sheriff asked casually.

After a dramatic pause, Sam shifted his eyes to Mark. "Make up yer mind, Sheriff. Are you asking me where I was last night or this morning?"

The sheriff couldn't stand this guy and he certainly wasn't feeling like playing games. He took a deep breath, maintaining eye contact with Sam, and rephrased the question. "Last night, Sam. Tell me about your night."

"Am I being questioned for something?" Sam asked, again belligerent.

"I would say that was a question, yes," said the sheriff. Mark turned to Christopher, "Did that sound like a question to you, Deputy?"

Christopher responded, "Oh most definitely. But maybe what Mr. Graber is saying is that he'd rather come to the station to tell us about where he was last night."

The sheriff turned back to Sam, "Is that true, Sam? You want to come down to the station to chat?"

Sam scoffed. "What is this? You two gonna play good cop, bad cop now?" He chuckled.

The sheriff squinted his eyes and began to speak again, "I just want to know…"

Sam interrupted him. "I know why you're here," he said, flicking his cigarette butt on the ground. "You think I started that fire last week." He stopped and licked his lips and stepped forward. "Well, you're wrong," he hissed. "I ain't got nothin' to do with that. I know they all think I did it, well, because those people are not exactly my friends, if ya get what I mean. And trust me, a few of 'em have definitely given me reasons to seek some revenge on 'em. But," he paused, "it wasn't me. And because of that, you're not gonna be able to prove it."

Mark waited for him to continue. He hoped Sam would put his foot in his mouth.

"Why would I want to burn their stupid barn down, anyway? If I wanted to hurt 'em, I'd do better than that," Sam said. He snorted and sent a ball of spit onto the ground next to him.

"Is that a threat?" The sheriff hoped to provoke some sort of confession.

"Hell no, that ain't a threat. You think I'm stupid enough to threaten somebody in front of two lawmen?" His voice remained calm and casual. "I'll tell ya again, you're wasting your time with me. I ain't the one you're looking for."

The deputy prodded him, "You know who did it, then?"

"Nope," Samuel said, staring hard at Christopher. "I don't have the foggiest idea."

Mark couldn't tell if Sam knew anything or not, but he could tell that they would get nowhere with this. He interjected, "Well, Sam, we sure do thank you for your time." This time, Mark wore the sarcastic grin. "You know where to find us if you ever want to confess or roll over on one of your friends." He winked and tipped his hat before he and Christopher walked back to the car. As Mark turned over the engine, he watched Sam light another cigarette.

"Well, he's an interesting guy," Christopher said. "You'll have to catch me up on his story sometime."

"Yeah, he and I go way back" the sheriff grumbled as he backed up the car and headed back to the station. "Let's send that note out for prints. We've got to sort this out and soon. I think we're going to need to pull out our secret weapon."

"What's the secret weapon?" Christopher asked.

"The sisters," Mark replied as he turned onto the highway.

Chapter Fourteen

"There are few things that compare to a barn raising in Spring," Beth said to Anna as the Schwartz home bustled with women of all ages working together to set a breakfast feast to be ready when the hardworking men outside needed some refreshment. Tables were set up outside close to the house, under the shade of the oak trees. The men had spent the early hours of the day removing the rubble from the fire and prepping the foundation for a new barn. Piles of stacked lumber and supplies were laid neatly off to the side, and the men worked in orderly fashion, combining their talents to complement each other. Noah and Jacob were in charge of the build, and Beth loved how they communicated what they needed from each person with respect, positivity and grace. There was so much love that went into a barn build and so much gratitude from those on the receiving end.

For this particular barn build, Beth couldn't help but think about how perfectly aligned it was with the season. Springtime brought a sense of renewal and the new barn would do the same for the Schwartz family. However, already into mid-morning, there was an energy that was hanging over the community that differed from anything Little Valley had ever experienced, for as long as Beth could remember. It was a sense of unrest.

Jacob had confessed to the community the mistakes he had made with Sam Graber, and although the elders and the bishop had decided that Jacob would be forgiven and the Schwartz family could stay, the community members had become concerned. With the recent second fire, an unsettling fear had spread like wildfire. Discussion of families moving away, finding homes in a safer town where they would feel more accepted and welcome, had moved outside of private homes and was being shared among each other.

Beth knew she was one of the few that wanted to stay. Little Valley was her home. She loved her life there, including her community and her English friends, too. But, in the past week, both her daughter Abigail and her own twin sister had confided in her that they were considering moving. It broke her heart to hear her loved ones talk about leaving, and she was determined to convince them to stay.

Beth and Anna took a seat at one of the picnic tables, sitting across from each other. They each had a cup of hot coffee and shared a danish. "How are you doing this morning?" Anna asked her sister.

"I'm enjoying this beautiful weather we are having," answered Beth. "It has turned out to be a perfect day for the Schwartz barn build, thank *Gotte*."

"*Ja*, it really has. Little Valley does have beautiful spring seasons," Anna said.

"This danish is quite good, *Schwester*. I think we may have perfected the recipe." Beth changed the subject, sensing that her sister was patronizing her. When Anna had mentioned the possibility of moving, Beth had cried and pleaded with her to change her mind. She couldn't stand the thought of living apart, and she informed Anna that she would not be leaving Little Valley. Anna had mentioned this once before and Beth had thought it was resolved, packed away for good. She was upset that Anna had not let it go and was reconsidering such an absurd idea.

Moments later, Rachel Schwartz approached the table and asked, "May I join you two?" She set a cup of tea down on the table next to Beth.

"*Ja*, of course," said Beth, patting the seat next to her on the bench and pushing the remaining danish her way. "You must try this! It is our newest recipe."

Rachel sat down and reached for a fork to grab a bite. "Mmmm... it is SO good! The two of you make the most delicious treats!"

"Please, finish it," encouraged Anna. "I've had more than my share of food this morning," she chuckled.

"Me too," said Beth, patting her stomach. "I can't keep eating like this," she said, chuckling as well.

Rachel finished the danish in two more bites and after taking a sip of her tea and setting her fork down, she said, "I can't thank you two enough for helping plan this day. I haven't been on the receiving end of a barn raising in many years, and it brings back happy memories to replace the sad ones." She paused, blinking away tears, and said, "So, *denki*, Anna and Beth. And Beth, Noah has been so *wunderbaar*. He has helped Jacob so much."

"You don't have to thank us, Rachel," Beth said, reaching out and touching Rachel's arm gently. "We are all part of a family here in Little Valley. We support you and are here for you, Jacob, and of course, Grace."

Rachel smiled and said, "You are so kind." She paused and looked at her hands in her lap. "I know Jacob has brought so much heartache to this community with his actions. If there is anything he or I can do to fix things, I hope you know that we will do it. We will do anything to make it right and to make all this fear go away. We pray to *Gotte* every day for wisdom, but the elders... and the sheriff... they all say to leave well enough alone and leave it up to them. Did you know that the bishop and the elders are talking about handing over some of our beloved land to that awful man? Poor Jacob would feel just terrible if it came to that." A tear trickled down her cheek as she continued, "And we were so guilt-ridden and heartbroken when we learned of the fire at the Fletcher home. Will it ever stop?" Rachel rested her head in her hands, her elbows propped on the table. Her shoulders moved rhythmically as she cried quietly.

"It's ok, Rachel. It's going to be ok," Beth said, gently patting her back.

"Rachel, please do not worry. *Ja*, it's true that Jacob made some mistakes and got mixed up with the wrong people, but if there is anything that Beth and I know, it's that the person behind the crime is not always who you think it is." Anna and Beth locked eyes. "Beth and I are going to do some investigating on our own and see if we can get to the bottom of this before any rash decisions are made or any other fires are started." The sisters continued to look in each other's eyes, as if they were communicating without words. "We've proven to be quite good at getting to the bottom of things like this," she chuckled.

Beth knew Anna was attempting to lighten the mood, but she also knew her sister was dead serious about it being time for them to get involved. Beth felt the all-too-familiar stomach uneasiness that resulted from the perfect mixture of excitement, anxiety and a tinge of fear. She looked across the table at her sister, her mirror image. Anna was right. It *was* time that the two of them, known well as the wise women of the community, stepped up to the plate and stopped this crime, too.

And maybe, just maybe, thought Beth, *we can convince everyone to stay in beautiful Little Valley.*

Chapter Fifteen

The Amish Inn stood tall, the late morning sun peeking out from behind the arched roof. Anna and Beth pulled up to the front, but they hesitated before stepping out of the buggy.

Looking straight ahead, they simultaneously reached out for each other's hand and squeezed tight. Ever since they were little girls, they would hold hands whenever they were facing something that made them feel uneasy in any way. Joining their hands brought them comfort and strength through connection.

"Alright, let's talk about what we're doing here," said Anna. "Remember, the sheriff thinks we can build trust with Hank and maybe get him to talk. This will be our first time to go undercover - I think that's what they call it."

"Right," Beth said, nodding her head. Her heart was racing. "The main goal is to get Hank to trust us enough to uncover some type of evidence."

"Ok, so we have to walk in here with an open mind, and be friendly," Anna said.

"I'm ready, if you're ready," Beth said, turning to look at Anna and giving her hand one last squeeze.

"I'm ready," said Anna, grabbing the box of cookies they had prepared to present as a gift.

After tying the reins to one of the white picket fence posts, the two women walked up the porch steps and entered the front door. A welcoming scent of cinnamon hung in the air. Beth and Anna were silent as they looked around the room. There were two tall-backed upholstered chairs set on either side of what looked like a very comfortable loveseat on one wall. A matching couch sat against the opposite wall, a coffee table centered in front of the couch. A crocheted blanket was thrown over the back of the couch and a handmade patchwork quilt hung on the wall. There was a wood-burning stove across the room, a perfectly stacked pile of logs sat on the hearth next to it.

An oil lamp sat on a round table by the door. Small wooden carved figurines of horses and faceless people dressed in traditional clothing were set on end tables and shelves around the room. The coffee table held a vase of fresh flowers and a hand-carved candle.

The sisters were in awe as they soaked in all the details. They weren't sure exactly how to feel as they surveyed the room. It almost felt like they were in a strange museum full of things that represented their lives, but yet it didn't feel authentic. All the decor was clearly made by people in their community, but it would actually be odd to see a home decorated in this manner in their community.

Hank appeared in one of the internal doorways, surprised to see the sisters standing in the front room. "Well, well, well, isn't this a nice surprise?" Hank said, sounding friendly.

"Hi, Mr. Davis," Anna returned his greeting cheerily. Beth began to fidget, smoothing her apron and checking for any loose strands of hair that may have fallen out of her *kapp*.

"Please call me Hank. And forgive me, but are you Mrs. Miller or Mrs. Troyer?" Hank asked Anna politely.

Beth stepped forward. "I'm Mrs. Troyer, Hank, but you can call me Beth."

"And I'm Anna Miller," said Anna.

"Ah. Well, it's nice to see you both," Hank responded with a smile. Beth couldn't help but take note of how friendly he was. The Hank that everyone knew was never this nice, so she was suspicious. But she was also willing to play along. "What brings you by today?" Hank asked the sisters.

"We wanted to see the new place and bring some of our sugar cookies for you and your guests as a grand opening gift." Anna responded with a warm smile. She handed the box to Hank.

"Oh, thank you!" Hank said as he peeked in the box. "I'm sure these are delicious. You two have quite the reputation around here for your desserts, you know."

The sisters smiled and there was a few seconds of awkward silence before Beth spoke, "So, how is business going? Have you had any new guests yet?"

Hank responded, "Oh yes, we have a couple visiting us now - they are out shopping and sightseeing. But we have had someone every night since we opened and we have bookings a few months out, as well. Our customers are fascinated with the Amish, er, your wonderful way of life." He stumbled over his words. "Can I show you around? The place isn't that big, but me and my team have put a lot of work into it and I would love to know what you think," he said enthusiastically.

"That would be great, thank you," Beth responded. She hoped she didn't sound as eager as she felt. She had become intrigued, she wanted to see more of what the fascination was with the Amish Inn.

Anna and Beth followed Hank to the back part of the inn where he showed them the vacant rooms. There were detailed panels with wainscotting on the walls and elaborately carved wooden bed frames. Beth chuckled to herself. Although the Amish create beautiful pieces like that for *Englishers*, it would actually be very rare to find such decor in a traditional Amish home. The Amish lived simple lives based on their faith, and it would be unusual to find such elegance in the homes of anyone in their community.

After seeing the rooms, Hank led them back through the front room and into the kitchen. "Last but not least," he said, "I would like to introduce you to the chef that makes all the delicious Amish meals for our guests. Ryan Green, this is Anna Miller and Beth Troyer."

Ryan was chopping onions on a large cutting board. She looked up without stopping and said, "Nice to meet you." Her voice was deep and less than enthusiastic. Ground beef was cooking in the skillet on the stove next to her. She set the knife down to stir the beef, breaking it up into smaller pieces.

"Nice to meet you, too," Anna said politely. Beth was uncomfortable with the thick tension that filled the room.

Hank seemed a bit embarrassed by Ryan's lack of welcome and said, "Beth and Anna brought us some of their sugar cookies, Ryan. These ladies sell their wonderful baked goods at the farmers' market each weekend. They are quite popular." He walked over and set the box down on the counter next to the sink.

"I'm excited to try them," Ryan said, barely louder than a mumble. She returned to chopping onions and said, "I'm sure they're great. Hank here will probably expect me to replicate them."

It didn't take a wise woman to see that Ryan was not a big fan of Hank. *This could work in our favor*, she thought to herself. Finding her voice, she asked Ryan, "Are you from around here?"

Ryan added the onions to the ground beef and stirred the mixture, turning the knob on the stove just a fraction to lower the temperature. She grabbed a bulb of garlic off the counter and used the side of her knife to break it into cloves. Without looking up, she responded while dicing the cloves of garlic. "I'm actually from Little Valley originally. I left to go to college years ago. I tried to make it as an artist, but it didn't pay enough to support me, so I went to culinary school instead." She added the diced garlic to the meat and returned to stirring it. She looked up and continued, "I came back because my mother is sick."

Before the sisters could react, Ryan continued. She patted Hank on the back roughly and raised her voice as she spoke. "And that's when I landed this awesome job here at the ol' Amish Inn. Isn't that right, Hank?" A sarcastic smile spread across her face.

Hank appeared to be frustrated and headed toward the back door. "I almost forgot to show you two the back patio. It's not quite done..." his voice trailed off as he headed out the back door, expecting the sisters to follow him.

Anna quickly followed with Beth close behind. Beth stopped before closing the storm door, and said, "It was nice to meet you, Ryan. If you're ever at the farmers' market, make sure you stop by our booth."

Ryan waved her hand in the air in a half-hearted goodbye, her back turned away from Beth. She returned to her cooking, stirring a can of crushed tomatoes into the skillet.

When Beth caught up to Anna and Hank, she could hear Hank's explanation that the back patio was almost ready for guests, but not quite. "I still need to build a fence to block the view of the shop next door." He motioned toward Nichols Garage, situated right next to the Amish Inn.

"Yes," Anna chuckled, "that is certainly not something you would see in an Amish community."

Chapter Sixteen

Noah sat at the table and watched as Beth floated around the kitchen cleaning every single surface. When Beth fell into a cleaning frenzy, it was usually because she was anxious, or she was excited. Today, she was excited, and her energy was contagious.

"It feels like a holiday, doesn't it?" Noah asked Beth, a broad grin spread across his face.

"*Ja*, it does. I can't wait to see everyone today!" Beth squealed with excitement. Her cousin's daughter, Eva Zook, had arrived just yesterday and all the Troyer kids were coming home to welcome her. "I was so surprised that everyone was available to visit on the same day. Peter and Faith both said they could make it around noon. Amos will be a little later, but he said he'll be here. Jonah's definitely coming, and there's no telling when Abigail will arrive. You know how Abigail is always late to everything." Beth chuckled. "I know everyone is so busy, but it feels like it has been forever since we've all been together."

Amos was Beth's second son, Peter was her oldest son, and Faith, her youngest daughter. Amos, Peter and Faith and their families came home for Sunday dinners regularly, but it was rare for everyone's schedules to align with Abigail's and Jonah's, too, like they did today.

"It will be quite the crowd, indeed. It's a good thing the weather is nice. We can gather outside and let the kids play," Noah said, sipping his coffee. "How was Eva's trip, by the way? Is she feeling settled?"

Right at that moment, Eva walked in the door looking fresh as a daisy with her lavender dress and white apron. Her blonde hair was tucked away neatly in her *kapp*. "*Ja*, I slept like a baby," Eva said, laughing. "*Gute mariye*! Can I help with anything?" She asked Beth, walking towards the sink to grab a cloth.

"Oh no," Beth answered quickly with a smile. "Please, sit and eat some breakfast. I know you must still be tired from traveling."

"*Gute mariye*," Noah said. "It is nice to see you this morning."

"*Denki* to both of you. It is so exciting to finally be here. I have looked forward to this for many months," Eva said. "Little Valley certainly is a beautiful town. I have dreamed of living here ever since I visited as a young girl."

"How are your parents?" Noah asked.

Eva sat and poured herself a cup of coffee from the coffee pot on the table. She scooped a teaspoon of sugar and added a drop of cream, stirring before taking a sip. "They are both well, *denki* for asking. *Maem* is a bit heartbroken that I have left Worthton, but she adores Beth and Anna and hopes to visit soon. *Dat* stays busy with the farm. They send their love."

"I am glad to hear they are well, and I know that Beth and Anna are happy to have you. As you know, they are both very talented bakers, so I am sure you will learn a lot from them." Noah stood and stretched, his arm reached high and his back arched. "Now, if you'll excuse me, I have yard chores for myself this morning. With the beautiful Spring, we have new grass to mow and flowers to tend to."

"Jonah said he is coming by earlier today to speak with you, *lieb*. I'm sure he can help with the yard, too, while he's here," Beth said.

"Oh, that will be *gut*. *Denki* for breakfast, dear." Noah said. He pulled on his work boots and his straw hat and headed out the back door.

Beth rinsed her rag, wrung it and folded it neatly, setting it down on the counter next to the sink. She sat down next to Eva and poured herself another cup of coffee.

"It smells *wunderbaar* in here, Beth," said Eva. "*Denki* again for having me here. I don't want to be a burden, so please let me help wherever I can."

There was a soft knock at the back door, and Anna entered. "*Hallo?*" Anna called out, her voice cheery.

"*Gute mariye!*" Beth greeted her sister.

"Ah, *gute mariye*, Anna!" Eva said, jumping up to give her a hug.

"Well, I'll say that you have grown quite a bit since I last saw you!" Anna said, laughing. "*Wie bischt?* How is your mother? Tell me about your trip!"

Anna sat down at the table, and the room soon filled with excited chatter. Eva recounted her experiences traveling from Worthton. She shared her excitement to learn everything she can from Anna and Beth. She talked about how she had mastered making fudge but needed help with pastries and pie crusts. "I have big dreams to open a bakery right here in Little Valley one day," Eva said, her eyes lit up as she spoke about it.

Anna and Beth exchanged glances. "Oh, that does sound exciting," said Beth. She and Anna had been asked on numerous occasions when they were going to open a bakery, but they loved the idea of keeping things simple with their booth at the farmers' market. And in their generation, a young woman opening a business of her own would push the boundaries in the community. Eva's generation, however, was quite different. Beth wondered why Eva had not yet married, but she would have plenty of time to dive into Eva's story in the upcoming months.

The sound of a horse and buggy arriving distracted Beth. She jumped up muttering, "Oh, excuse me, please. That must be Jonah." She rushed to the front door, swung it open and squealed, "Jonah!" She was always so excited to see her youngest son, and today was no exception. She greeted her son with a big bear hug. Jonah returned the hug, his strong arms and broad shoulders wrapped tight around his mother, lifting her off her feet for a brief second. Beth laughed and said, "*Gute mariye, sohn!* Please come in and say hello to your cousin, Eva. She just arrived in Little Valley last night."

Jonah followed Beth into the house and greeted Eva. He was a few years younger than her and had no recollection of her visit years ago. "*Gute mariye*, Aunt Anna," he said. Then, with a tip of his hat, he greeted Eva. "It's *gut* to meet you, Eva. I know my *maem* is very excited to have you visiting."

Anna stood and gave Jonah a hug. "*Ja*, it has been very quiet around here since Jonah left. He was the baby and the last to leave the coop."

Eva said, "The last time I saw you, you were just a toddler. I think maybe just learning to walk. You've definitely changed." They all laughed together and spent the next few minutes chatting about the weather and catching up with each other's lives before Jonah excused himself to go find his father and lend a helping hand. Beth followed him out the door, promising Anna and Eva that she would be back in just a few minutes.

Pushing open the back door, Jonah almost ran right into Noah who had seen Jonah's buggy and was headed inside the house to greet him. Noah's face lit up when he saw his son, and the two embraced. "It's so *gut* to see you, *sohn!*" Noah's voice boomed, filled with happiness. Beth stood by to relish the moment of seeing the two reunite again. Her heart was full.

"Same here, *dat*," said Jonah, and then as if he just remembered something, he continued. "Oh! I'm glad I have you both together. I have some news to share, and I wanted to tell you both at the same time."

Beth bounced up and down, her hands clasped in front of her chest, "Oh! I'm so excited! What is it, Jonah?"

"Here, let's sit," said Noah, and the three settled on the seats of the picnic table just a few steps beyond the back porch.

Beth leaned in as Jonah began to speak, his thumb hooked in his suspenders by his chest, his back straight. Even though Jonah was a young man now, at age twenty, sometimes she still saw that toddler Eva was just referring to when she looked at him. Anna said Jonah was the baby, and she was right. He was her baby, and she adored him.

"Well, my big news is that I got a job offer that I am actually really excited about," Jonah said.

Beth threw her arms around her son, exclaiming, "That's great, Jonah! *Gotte* is *gut!*"

Noah smiled, "Congratulations, *sohn*. What is the job?" Beth knew Noah was holding his breath waiting to hear if Jonah would be working with wood as he had dreamed.

"Well, it's a bit of a variety. I'll be a sort of handyman, fixing things." Jonah's face beamed with pride.

"That's *wunderbaar!*" Noah reached over to give his son a loving pat on the back. "I'm very proud of you, and I know you will be very successful."

Jonah smiled from ear to ear. "*Denki, Dat.* Your words mean the world to me."

Beth interjected, "So, where is this *wunderbaar* job?" She asked, excited to hear more.

"It's in town, at the new Amish Inn," Jonah replied. Silence fell over the table. The smiles disappeared from Beth and Noah's faces as they exchanged worried looks.

Chapter Seventeen

"I can't believe it," said Beth, wringing her hands and pacing the kitchen floor. "Thank *Gotte* that Eli was up early enough to extinguish the fire before it blazed high."

"*Ja,*" Noah said, his head hung, and his shoulders slouched. "This has to stop. When is enough going to be enough? We can't keep going like this."

"I need to go see Anna," said Beth. "Why don't you go back to bed and get a bit more rest. I'll just be gone a little while, and I can wake you when I return."

Noah agreed and dragged himself back off to bed, his feet shuffling as he walked. Beth watched him walk away and then quickly threw a shawl over her shoulders before heading out the back door. *I wonder if I should lock the door?* That thought had never crossed her mind until now, but she was scared. The fires had hit too close to home this time with Eli's barn being the target. She knew Anna was frantic, and Beth wanted to help console her.

Beth knocked softly on the back door of Anna's home and turned the knob. The door creaked open, and Beth could see a light flickering from a candle in the front living room. She called out to her sister softly, "Anna?"

Anna answered, "*Ja, Schwester*, I'm here."

Beth entered the living room to find Anna rocking back and forth slowly in her rocking chair. Her hands were holding crochet needles, the blanket was laid out in her lap, and her hands moving rhythmically. Her cheeks were wet from tears and her eyes were red.

Beth sat down on the couch close to her sister and leaned forward, reaching out to hold her sister's hand. "It's ok, *Schwester*," Beth said softly. "I know that was so scary."

A new tear slid down Anna's cheek. She set the crochet needles down and held Beth's hand cupped in hers. Her face was still turned down when she said, "*Denki, Schwest-*

er, for coming over. I just don't know how I could do life without you."

Beth wiped away a tear with her free hand and said, "Of course, Anna. I am always going to be here for you." Then, after a brief pause, she asked, "How is Eli? Is he able to rest?"

"*Ja*," Anna nodded. "I gave him some chamomile tea, and he is resting now."

"I'm so sorry this happened, Anna," said Beth, squeezing her sister's hand.

"Me, too," said Anna. "Me, too." She paused and reached with her right hand to blow her nose with her handkerchief. She squeezed Beth's hand back and then released it. Beth leaned back and Anna returned to crocheting. There was a moment of silence as the two women sat there together in the dim light.

"What are you thinking, *Schwester*? Do you know how it started? Did Eli see anything?" Beth asked, her mind racing with questions now that things had finally settled down and she could think.

Anna spoke without looking up, "*Ja*, Eli said he saw Sam Graber's truck leaving the property after the fire was started."

"What?" Beth couldn't believe how calm Anna sounded. "Are you sure?" she asked.

"*Ja,* he is sure. Sam is the only one in town that drives that ugly bright yellow truck. It's so bright that Eli could even see it in the early dawn." Anna spoke with no emotion, as if she were bored. The tone of her voice worried Beth.

Anna continued, "I don't know how we can stay in Little Valley after this. I don't think this is ever going to stop, and I can't live in constant fear."

Beth sat quietly. Anna was upset, and with good reason. She was sure that she would come to her senses after some time and rest. If there was one thing she knew about her twin sister, it's that she didn't give up.

"I know you want to stay, Beth, but I need you. Promise me, *Schwester*, that you'll consider moving with us to a safer community?" Anna's hand rested in her lap, her face turned to her sister, her eyes wet with tears. Beth knew what she needed to hear, but she couldn't lie to her sister, and she had no intention of leaving Little Valley.

"We need to find out who did this, *Schwester*," Beth said, avoiding the question her sister had asked. "Let me think."

Anna sighed. Beth knew she was defeated, and she needed to figure out how to bring her back. It was only hours earlier that Beth's children and their families visited. Anna and Eli were over at the house, too, and everyone was laughing, playing, smiling, and happiness filled the air.

Beth would not let someone ruin all of that for them, but she needed her sister to help find the evidence they needed for the sheriff to arrest Sam.

"The sheriff!" said Beth, with a loud whisper. She was careful not to speak too loudly. She didn't want to disturb Eli. "Does Sheriff Streen know about this yet?"

Anna shook her head. "No, of course not. It's still early, and Eli and Noah were able to put the fire out themselves, thank *Gotte*."

"Well, we're going to have to go tell him about all of this right away this morning," Beth said. "Maybe there is another clue left behind this time," Beth was hopeful. "There has to be something we're missing."

Anna nodded, and the women fell silent again. Anna stopped crocheting, gathered the blanket, needles and yarn and set them aside in the wicker basket on the floor next to her. She blew her nose again and grabbed a clean handkerchief off the table next to her, wiping the tears off her face.

Beth sat still, waiting to see what Anna was going to do next.

"The sun is starting to shine now. Shall we have a cup of tea, *Schwester*?" Anna smiled a half-smile at Beth and reached out for her hand again. The two rose to their feet together, straightening their tired backs. Leaning into each other, the sisters threw their arms around each other for a long tight hug before pulling back. Standing face to face, their hands clasped together again, Beth said, "I love you, *Schwester.*" A tear slid down her cheek.

Anna wiped Beth's tear away and smiled. "I love you, too, Beth. *Denki* for being here," Anna said. "Now let's stop crying, go have some tea, and talk about what we need to do to put this criminal behind bars."

Chapter Eighteen

"I am so sorry, Anna," said Sheriff Streen. "I hate that this happened to you and Eli. And I am so relieved that Eli and Noah were able to catch it before much damage was done."

Mark sat behind his desk, still drinking his first cup of coffee. Anna and Beth were sitting in the guest chairs placed side by side, facing him. The front door swung open as Deputy Jones entered briskly.

"Oh my gosh, I'm late. My apologies. The kids were troublesome..." he stopped mid-sentence and greeted the women, removing his hat. He nodded at the sheriff and said, "I hope this is just a friendly visit and that everything is ok?" He pulled his desk chair over to the edge of the sheriff's desk, paper and pen in hand.

"I'm afraid not," Mark answered, rubbing his forehead as if he were suffering from a headache. "There was another fire started last night, well, early morning, it sounds like. This time it was at Anna's house. Her husband, Eli, caught it quick enough and was able to extinguish it before any real damage happened. But here's the kicker: Eli caught a glimpse of Sam Graber's yellow truck pulling off the property."

"Ok," said Christopher, taking notes. When he looked up, he said to the group, "Well, I guess it's something that we have the truck ID now."

Mark nodded, but he exhaled. "Unfortunately, I don't think that's going to be enough. We need more than that. We sent the notes off for fingerprints," Mark pulled a plastic bag containing the notes out of the drawer and dropped them on the table in front of Anna and Beth, "but nothing matched criminal records." He stopped abruptly and asked, "You didn't get a note tacked to your door, did you, Anna?"

Anna shook her head. Beth reached out to examine the notes. The paper was thick, a little heavier weight than normal, and the writing was immaculate, almost perfect print. The question mark matched on each note and was unique, with a curly curve at the top that had an elegant style. Beth passed the notes over to Anna to review as well.

The sheriff continued, "We spoke with Archer, the bartender at Sam's pub. He told us about a conversation that Sam and Hank had where Hank was basically asking Sam to leave y'all alone, but Archer says that Sam never actually admitted starting the fires. He told us that Sam did threaten y'all, but said that he would do way worse than set your barns on fire."

"Which is what he told us, too," Christopher said.

The sisters exchanged worried looks. Anna spoke up, "So you don't think Sam Graber is responsible for the fires?"

Beth chimed in, "Well, if he didn't do it, who did? Who else could want to harm us like this?" She paused briefly, "Do you suspect Hank Davis at all?" She braced herself for the answer. She and Noah were so worried about Jonah starting work with Hank, and she hoped Hank was not behind all of this.

Mark shook his head, "No, I don't think it's Hank. I know Sam is behind this. I just have a gut feeling about it, and there's really no other explanation." He ran his hand through his hair. "We just have to get some circumstantial evidence so we can finally lock him up."

Anna interjected, "I agree with the sheriff about Hank. Our son-in-law, Moses, said he came into the hardware store just the other day and bought some supplies. He said he was really friendly and mentioned that things had started off on the wrong foot, that he wanted to make peace with our community." She turned to Beth, "And then you and I had a pleasant experience with him when we went to the inn the other day, too."

Beth nodded. "It's true," she said, "but I'm still not sure if we can fully trust him. He actually just hired my son, Jonah, to work as his handyman. He starts tomorrow, so I think we should pay the inn another visit to check on things."

Anna agreed. "*Gut* idea, Beth. Plus, we could go pay Shannon Graber a visit, too. She has always been so kind to us..."

Beth interrupted, "*Ja*! We actually have to deliver her cookie order, so that's perfect!" Beth was sitting on the edge of her seat, her leg bouncing up and down as if her body was about to explode with excitement.

Mark chimed in, "Excellent!" He smiled at the sisters, a sense of hope hanging in the air. He turned to Christopher, "Ok, so Anna and Beth will visit Sam's mother and the inn. You and I will go pay another visit to Sam and find out why - and how - Eli could've seen his truck this morning. Ladies, please let us know what you find out, if anything. And please," the sheriff stopped and leaned forward with a serious expression, "*please* be safe. We do not want you to put yourselves in danger. Promise us you will stay safe?"

The sisters smiled angelically and nodded in agreement.

Chapter Nineteen

Shannon Graber answered the door just seconds after Anna and Beth knocked. She let out a small squeak of excitement when she saw the two women standing on her doorstep.

"I'm so excited to see you two! Please say you'll come in this time!" She held the door wide open and motioned for Anna and Beth to enter her home. "I simply won't take no for an answer," she said. She smiled and sounded cheery, but Beth immediately felt something wasn't right.

"Thank you, Shannon! We would love to come in and chat for a few minutes. That's very kind," Anna said, returning the warm greeting.

Beth smiled in agreement. "You have such a beautiful house," she said. Complimenting one's home is not traditional of the Amish, but Beth knew it meant a lot to *Englishers* and she wanted Shannon to trust them.

"Aw, thank you so much. Please have a seat, but then remind me who is who. I am so sorry. I know you must get asked that all the time, but I really can't tell the two of you apart!" Shannon asked kindly.

Anna and Beth took a seat at Shannon's large dining room table. It was wooden with a heavy coat of lacquer giving it an unnatural shine. The chairs were almost designed to look regal, with a fancy design carved into the top of the tall back of each, floral upholstered material covering the seats. The sisters sat on one side of the table, with Shannon directly across from them. Behind Shannon was an oversized china cabinet filled with royal blue and white porcelain dishes. Matching blue goblet glasses were on display as well as a variety of small crystal figurines.

When Beth shifted her eyes back to Shannon, she realized that Shannon, sitting perfectly under a ray of sun shining through the large picture windows behind the sisters, looked pale. *That's what is different,* thought Beth.

She wondered if maybe Shannon just wasn't wearing as much makeup as she would normally wear when the sisters had seen her at the farmers' market.

On the table between them, sat a beautiful china tea set. "Oh, this is very pretty," said Beth, as Shannon handed her a dainty small cup and a saucer. The cup was filled with an aromatic tea. Beth closed her eyes and held the cup under her nose, trying to distinguish the scent floating above her cup.

As if Anna read her mind, she asked Shannon, "What type of tea is this? It smells absolutely wonderful."

Shannon smiled and responded, "It's actually my favorite. It's a vanilla chai tea. Have you ever had chai tea before?"

"I'm not sure that I have," said Beth, "but it is delicious. I can taste a blend of cinnamon and clove, I think."

Anna agreed, "Yes, it is very good. I think maybe there is cardamom spice, as well? It is very unique."

Shannon chuckled, "That's right! All of that blended together, plus I think there is also nutmeg and a touch of ginger. And of course, the vanilla adds the extra sweetness. It makes me so happy that I can introduce a new tea to you!"

"Well, it certainly makes us happy, too!" Beth said with a wink. She and Anna laughed along with Shannon.

"How is your day going, Shannon?" Anna asked before taking another sip.

"Not too bad," Shannon said. "How about you two?"

"Oh, we're busy, as usual. Our younger cousin is visiting from Worthton and we are spending a lot of time with her getting her settled in and teaching her our recipes. She wants to be a baker, and she dreams of opening a bakery one day." Beth shared with Shannon, hoping to steer the conversation to families.

"That's wonderful!" Shannon exclaimed. "You know, my daughter went to culinary school."

"Oh?" Anna said, "I didn't realize you had a daughter."

"Oh yes. She is actually a better artist than she is a cook, but she is making more money as a cook, that's for sure." Shannon scoffed, her eyebrows raised and then relaxed again.

A feeling of Deja vu swept over Beth. She knew she had recently had a similar conversation with someone else about this same thing, but she couldn't place it.

Shannon continued, "Yeah, my kids never got along very well. My husband passed away years ago when they were young, and I had hoped they would grow up close. But things don't always turn out as you hope. My daughter and son, they're close in age, but they fought so much growing up. I knew that she couldn't wait to move away, so I let her go find her own path. Sammy, though, he stayed home with me. He and I were always very close. He is such a smart businessman, you know." Shannon's face beamed with pride.

Beth wondered how Shannon could see a completely different side of Sam Graber than the rest of the world, and she quickly pushed away doubt that maybe her kids were not who she thought they were.

A timer went off in the kitchen, and Shannon jumped up. "Oh, one minute. That's a reminder for myself that I have to take my medicine. I'll be right back." She left the room.

Beth and Anna exchanged glances but just seconds later, Shannon reappeared. "I'm so sorry about that."

"It's fine, Shannon," said Anna. "Is everything ok with your health?" She asked politely.

"Well, actually, I'm kind of embarrassed to admit it, but I told a tiny fib to you two the other day at the market." Shannon poured herself another cup of tea and topped off Beth and Anna's, as well, while continuing. "I mean, I'm totally fine, but I said that I was away visiting friends when I was actually in Wilsonville at the Wellness Institute there. I was diagnosed with cancer a few months ago, and I had to have some treatment there." Her words sped up, falling off her lips quickly. "But everything went very well, and they suspect I will go right into remission in no time."

"I'm so sorry, Shannon," said Anna. "We didn't know."

"Yes, we will definitely be praying for your body to heal quickly," Beth chimed in. "Please let us know if you need anything."

Shannon smiled at the women and said, "That is very nice of you both, but Sam and Ryan are taking good care of me. Ryan actually moved home, and she has a job now. Ironically, she's working at the new Amish Inn, making Amish cuisine! You just have to meet her! I'm sure she could learn so much from the both of you!"

Anna and Beth sat across from the table, stunned and speechless.

"Oh. We didn't realize.." Anna stuttered.

Beth jumped in, "We just met Ryan the other day, actually, when we visited the new inn. We had a tour of the place, and we had no idea that she was your daughter."

"Yes," said Anna, wanting to help, "that's right. She seemed very..." Her words trailed off as she looked to Beth for help to finish her sentence.

"Confident. She seemed very confident. Let's see, I think she was cooking something with beef that day we were there. It smelled so good." Beth squeezed Anna's hand under the table.

"Oh good! I'm glad you got to meet her. She hasn't made any friends here yet. Between us and the wall, I will say that she can be a hard person to like. She has held a grudge against me for years now. She always accuses me of favoring her brother over her, and it's just not true. I love my children equally, as I'm sure all parents do, right?" Shannon looked to the women for validation.

"Oh yes, that is true. And I don't think it's uncommon for one child to feel left out at times. I'm sure you are a wonderful mother." Anna responded.

Beth wanted to steer the conversation back to Sam, trying to stay focused on collecting evidence. "How has Sam been holding up since your diagnosis?"

"Oh, Sam is a strong man," Shannon said, a broad smile stretched from ear to ear. "He has really done well with the bar." She set down her cup and looked at both girls with softened eyes. "I know he has said some pretty terrible things about your families in the past, and I wish I could make that right, I honestly do. He blames your community for losing the table games which were bringing in a good chunk of money for him. I'm sure you can understand why he would be so upset about that." She paused half a beat before continuing, "But I promise you ladies that Sammy is a sweetheart. He wouldn't hurt a fly. It's kinda like what they say about small dogs, he's all bark and no bite." Her smile was back, but this time, Beth felt like it was a little forced. Or maybe it was just fake. She couldn't quite tell, but that uneasy feeling in her stomach was back, and she knew it was time to go.

Anna and Beth squeezed each other's hand under the table, pleasant smiles held fast on their faces.

"Thank you, Shannon, we will try to remember that," Anna said half-heartedly.

Beth nodded, "Thank you for such a lovely tea, but we should probably head out. We have a few errands left to run." She and Anna stood to leave.

"Oh, bummer! I feel like I talked about myself and my family the whole time. I didn't even get a chance to learn about you and your wonderful families." Shannon pleaded, "Please do come back again. I would love to get to know you better."

The twins thanked Shannon for inviting them in, and for the wonderful tea. They wished her good health and said they would see her next weekend at the market. They said everything but promises that they would return for more conversation. The sisters jumped into their buggy and headed home, sitting next to each other silently. Beth signaled her horse to pick up the pace. She and Anna needed to get home where they felt safe, so they could process all the information they just received.

Chapter Twenty

Beth and Anna had been lost in their own thoughts ever since they said goodbye to Shannon Graber. They drove straight back to Anna's house and started working silently side-by-side, setting the table for lunch. When the table was ready, the two sat down across from each other, making sandwiches for themselves. After taking a few bites, Beth started the conversation.

"Ok, so what just happened?" Beth said. "Can we take it piece by piece and try to make sense of all of this?"

Anna nodded, "*Ja*, I don't see any other way. That was just much more than I ever expected, honestly, but I don't think we got what we went for. That's the confusing, and frustrating, part."

"Oh, I know. I completely agree with you, *Schwester*, but let's see." Beth set her half-eaten sandwich on her plate. "First of all, let's start with Shannon. I can't believe she was diagnosed with cancer! That poor woman."

"Yes, but is she a nice lady? I think I am confused about that. The end of the conversation started to take a weird turn. I don't think we should start with Shannon." Anna said. She took her last bite.

"Ok, good point. Let's start with Ryan then. I know you were just as shocked as I was to find out that Ryan is Shannon's daughter." Beth said, raising an eyebrow at Anna.

"*Ja*, I was just as shocked as you were. I definitely was not expecting that," Anna said.

"So, what do we know about Ryan?" Beth held out her fist and started counting on her fingers, outstretching one finger at a time. "She and her mother do not get along. That's one."

Anna interrupted, "Maybe that explains why she didn't mention family names when she talked about her family at the inn."

Beth nodded.

Anna continued, "She and her brother do not get along. That's two."

Beth chuckled, "That is probably the least surprising part of this whole thing." Anna laughed out loud.

"Ryan works at the Amish Inn. That's three, but we knew that," Beth continued.

"Wait, back to number one. I don't know if it's important, but she blames her mom for a lot of things. And I didn't realize their father died when they were children, either. What number is that?" Anna said.

"Four. That's number four," Beth said.

"What else?" Anna asked.

"I think that's everything, right?" Beth said, genuinely wondering if they were forgetting something. "Now, let's move on to Sam since he was the whole reason we were there to begin with."

Anna nodded. "What did we learn about Sam? I'm trying to remember now, and I'm not having any luck."

"It feels like the only thing we learned is how much Shannon loves Sam, but did we already know that?" Beth asked, her forehead wrinkled in confusion.

"I think so. It became strange at the end of the conversation, though, right? Or am I imagining things?" Anna asked.

Beth responded quickly, "Oh no, that wasn't your imagination. What I can't figure out is either Shannon truly believes Sam is harmless," she held out another finger, and said slowly, "*or*, she wants *us* to believe that he is harmless."

Anna nodded. "*Ja*, that is the confusing part, but regardless, Eli saw his truck this morning. So, he's *not* harmless."

"*Ja*, I do feel like we're missing something. I think we're going to have to sleep on it." Beth said.

Anna took a deep breath and exhaled slowly, allowing her shoulders to drop and relax. "Let's talk about something else for a few minutes. I need to clear my head of all of this, or I won't sleep at all tonight."

"*Gut* idea, *Schwester*. This all feels very overwhelming. It feels like we are so close to the truth, but it's just out of reach. Maybe Sheriff Streen is arresting Sam right now, since he said he was going to go talk to him again today."

Anna put her hands together as if she were praying and turned her face up towards the ceiling. Beth chuckled.

Beth stood and cleared the table of their dirty dishes. "Let's go sit on the couch and relax. And you've got the right idea. Let's take a few minutes to pray over this and leave it in *Gotte's* hands for the rest of the day."

"*Ja*, that sounds *wunderbaar*," said Anna. She stood and stretched, groaning about feeling old. Beth grinned and said, "Don't forget we're the same age, *Schwester*. Watch what you say about being old." She winked at her sister.

"I said I *feel* old. I didn't say I *was* old," Anna laughed, "but we are definitely not as young as we used to be. My body, and my mind, remind me of that every day."

"Well, come on, old woman, let's go sit down, then," Beth teased her.

The sisters headed into the living room and relaxed next to each other on the couch. They held hands and bowed their heads in prayer. Anna began to pray, her voice level just above a whisper, "Dear Lord, give us the wisdom to help the good sheriff and deputy stop these fires from continuing. Bring peace to our town and our community. Protect us, Lord, from those who want to hurt us, and help us find forgiveness in our hearts as you forgive our sins. Help us to live a life of faith and purity and serve as an example to those around us, spreading your love to all." Anna paused and gave Beth's hand a gentle squeeze.

Beth continued the prayer, "Lord, please be with Shannon Graber as she battles her illness and with Ryan as she settles into Little Valley. Help her find what she is looking for, Lord, and help her to be kind to her mother. And with Sam, please help him find his way to your heart, Lord. And *denki* for my family, *Gotte*, and for this beautiful town we live in. For these things, we are forever grateful." Beth stopped and gave Anna's hand a gentle squeeze.

"Amen," Anna said.

"Amen," said Beth.

The two women opened their eyes and released their hands, leaning back on the soft cushions of the couch.

"I always feel better after praying with you, *Schwester*." Beth said, turning her face toward Anna.

"I do, too, *Schwester*. I do too." Anna said, as she smiled at her identical twin. "Now, you never did tell me about Matthew and Jessica. I'm so eager to hear about that. They are both such *wunderbaar* people."

"Oh, that's right!" Beth said, and she started to tell Anna about that day at the diner when she saw the two of them chatting. Before she could even say much at all, though, Beth looked over to see that Anna had fallen fast asleep. She stopped talking and covered her up with a warm blanket before sneaking quietly out the back door.

Chapter Twenty-One

B eth woke up with mixed feelings. She tossed and turned all night playing the conversation with Shannon over and over again in her head. The visit left her more confused, and she desperately wanted answers. On the flip side, though, she was excited to go visit Jonah on his first day on the job at the Amish Inn. She had decided that she was going to have faith that Hank Davis had made some positive changes and was going to treat Jonah with the respect that he deserved, so today's visit would be less about protecting Jonah and more about celebrating and supporting him.

Noah was spending the day helping Jacob again with his long list of orders, and Eva was spending her day with Abigail. Beth slipped on her shoes and headed over to her sister's house. Anna was watering her container plants outside on her back porch. One of the many things about her home in Little Valley that Beth loved was that her back porch had morning sun and her front porch had evening sun. It allowed for beautiful flowers to bloom in both places, and it worked the same for her sister whose house sat side-by-side with hers.

"*Gute mariye!*" she called out to Anna.

"*Ja, gute mariye* indeed," Anna returned the greeting. "I guess you already watered your plants this morning?"

"*Ja*, I was up early today," said Beth, walking up the porch steps.

"Everything ok?" Anna asked, checking in on her sister.

"*Ja*, I just didn't sleep well. Too much on my mind, I guess," Beth winked at her sister.

"Don't I know it," said Anna. "Well, come in and let's plan our day together."

Beth followed Anna into the house. "How's Eli this morning?" Beth asked. "I seriously can't even believe the fire was yesterday early morning. It feels like several days have passed already."

"I was thinking the same thing," said Anna, "but it still seems very fresh for Eli. He is like you. I'm not sure he slept much last night. He said every little sound had him on edge."

"Oh, that's *baremlich*. I will pray for him tonight," Beth said.

"Well, hopefully the sheriff has good news for us today," said Anna. "When are we headed out to see him?"

"I want to go see Jonah first, and then we'll catch up to the sheriff after that, if that's ok. I know Jonah is expecting me earlier in the day." Beth explained.

"*Ja*, that is fine. After all, he that knows patience, knows peace," Anna said to Beth with a wink. She knew Beth loved proverbs.

"Ooohh, that's one of my favorites! And perfect timing, *Schwester*!" Beth grinned.

Anna chuckled at her sister as she slipped on her shoes and straightened her *kapp*. "Shall we go?"

"*Ja*! I'm ready," Beth answered enthusiastically, heading for the door.

The sisters mounted the buggy, and Beth gave the signal for the horse to trot. On the drive to the Amish Inn, the sisters discussed the baked goods for the weekend's market.

"Has Jessica placed her order yet?" Beth asked Anna.

"Not yet, but I suspect it will be the same as the last two weeks," Anna said.

"We should stop by today and check in. I wanted to hear what she thought about the new strawberry cream cheese danishes, too." Beth said, keeping her eyes on the road in front of her as modern automobiles passed them.

"*Gut* idea," said Anna, "and maybe I'll get a sneak peek into the romance that's happening." The sisters laughed.

"I didn't get a chance to finish telling you about that," Beth said. "You fell asleep right after talking about how old you feel."

Anna knew Beth was teasing her, so she played along, "Well, maybe you need to work on your storytelling skills."

The two continued to banter and laugh the rest of the trip, pulling up in front of the Amish Inn in a light-hearted mood. They jumped down out of the buggy and after tying the reins to the same fencepost as a few days earlier, they walked up the porch steps and entered the front door. This time, there was a man, a woman and a young child sitting in the front room. When Anna and Beth walked in, the room fell silent and all eyes turned to them.

The sisters were not new to gawks and stares from the English, so they smiled and greeted them softly with Good Mornings as they passed by and headed into the back area. They found Jonah there, bent over the bathroom sink.

Beth whispered, "*Hallo*, Jonah."

Jonah spun around and said, "*Maem*! Aunt Anna! *Hallo*! Perfect timing. I need advice on how to get this sink unclogged. I've been working on it ever since I got here and nothing is working."

"*Ach du lieva*," said Anna, leaning in to take a closer look. "Let me see."

Jonah moved out of his aunt's way and smiled at his *maem*. "I'm so glad you came!"

Beth glowed. She loved feeling needed, and Jonah was so special to her. "*Wie bischt*? How's your first day going?" Beth asked.

Jonah leaned in and said, his voice lowered, "I think it's going really well. At least it was until I ran into this drain problem."

"You'll be fine," said Beth. She leaned towards Anna who was looking under the sink. Jonah had disassembled the piping, and the pieces laid on the floor next to the sink. Turning back to Jonah, she said, "... unless someone out there needs to use the restroom." She winked.

Anna stood up. "Ever since we put in the plumbing, I've had this issue off and on. I know just what to do, but Jonah, you'll have to put this back together first. The problem is further in the pipe, in the wall, or maybe even further. All we need is some baking soda and vinegar to flush it out after you put everything back together."

Jonah's expression showed relief. "Ok, I'll put it back together right now. *Denki, denki*, Aunt Anna."

"We'll go get the baking soda and vinegar and we'll be right back," Beth whispered to Jonah. Jonah nodded and sat down on the floor, quickly reinstalling the pipe methodically.

The sisters headed to the kitchen. They wondered if they would run into Ryan, but the kitchen was empty. Even the visitors in the front room were nowhere to be seen. It seemed as if the place was empty except for Anna, Beth and Jonah - *which is ironic since it is the Amish Inn*, Beth thought to herself with a chuckle. Beth and Anna started opening cabinets looking for the ingredients they needed. The women thought surely there would be baking soda and vinegar stored somewhere in the kitchen, and they were on a mission to find it.

Beth opened her third cabinet without luck when she heard Anna ask, "Wait. What is this?"

"Did you find it?" asked Beth, her head was deep into one of the lower cabinets, and she was sorting through the baking ingredients.

Anna didn't respond. Beth pulled her head out of the cabinet and looked up. Anna was standing on a wooden step stool holding what looked like a large pad of paper with binder rings at the top. Anna had flipped over the first page and Beth could see and read the words "Sketch Pad" on the cover, even though it was upside down.

"What is it, Anna?" Beth asked, standing up.

"It looks like a drawing of the Little Valley Pub building and some redesign plans," said Anna, sounding confused.

"Step down," Beth said, "and let me see it."

Anna stepped off the stool and set the pad down flat on the counter. There was a well-drawn image of Little Valley Pub but the word "Pub" was scratched out furiously. Below that drawing was a drawing of what looked like the inside of a fancy restaurant. There were tables covered in tablecloths with candles set in the center of each. The light fixtures looked very modern. The curtains on the windows were drawn to look like lace.

Beth turned the page. A drawing of what looked like the front of a restaurant menu had the words Sous un Arbre spelled across the type, printed immaculately. A tree was expertly drawn around the words. Beth and Anna did not recognize these words, but the beauty in the picture struck them. In the bottom corner of the paper, a question was printed neatly. It read, "Do I like this name?" The question mark had a distinct curly curve to it that Beth and Anna immediately recognized.

"*Ach du lieva*!" Beth whispered to Anna, closing the pad of paper. "Put this back exactly as you found it. We've got to go tell the sheriff. I think we solved the case!" Beth was bouncing up and down on her toes. Anna moved quickly to put the pad back exactly as she had found it. Beth opened the next cabinet below and found the box of baking soda and a bottle of vinegar. The sisters grabbed the food items and ran to find Jonah still assembling the pipe.

"I'm sorry, dear," Beth said, her voice was rushed, and she leaned over Jonah, "but we have to go. Something very important has just come up."

Anna interjected and said, "Listen carefully, Jonah. You need a pot of boiling water. You pour that down the drain first, then follow it with a cup of each of these." She placed the ingredients on the floor just outside the bathroom. "Then, cover the drain with a cloth for about 10 minutes and then pour another pot of water down the drain."

Jonah nodded, "Ok, I got it. *Denki*, Aunt Anna."

The sisters turned to leave, and Jacob said, "Wait!" They stopped and turned around.

Jonah asked, "Is everything ok?" He had a look of sincere concern on his face.

The sisters looked at each other, and then they looked back at Jonah. Beth answered him with an impish smile, "Actually, everything is really, really *gut*, Jonah. We'll see you later, *sohn*." Beth rushed back to give Jonah a kiss on the forehead before following Anna out the front door.

Chapter Twenty-Two

B eth untied the reins from the fencepost outside of the Amish Inn and jumped into the buggy next to Anna. She started to turn the horse when Anna yelled out, "Wait! Look!" Her finger was pointed in the direction of Nichols Garage next door to the inn.

Beth followed the direction of Anna's pointed finger, and a squeal escaped from her lips. "*Ach du lieva, Gotte is gut!*" She exclaimed, spotting the sheriff's car parked in the lot. She raised her eyes to the sky and said a silent, quick prayer of thanks. She signaled for her horse to head towards the garage next door instead of turning back the other way down Main Street.

Once in the Nichols Garage parking lot, the women jumped out of the buggy, leaving the horse untied and ran to find the sheriff. They found him in conversation with Wyatt Nichols, the garage owner. The deputy was standing next to the sheriff. Anna and Beth knew Wyatt from years ago when they were younger. They grew up in Little Valley together. Wyatt was always very respectful of the Amish community, and he would often say hello at the market when he was shopping, sometimes stopping to buy a treat.

As they approached the men, Anna and Beth could hear Sheriff Streen asking about Sam's truck. The sheriff say, "So Sam Graber says he left his truck here on Tuesday for an oil change..."

"Sheriff!" Anna called out before Wyatt could answer. The men turned to see Anna and Beth just a few feet away. There was a sense of urgency on both of their faces.

"Excuse me, Wyatt. Deputy, you want to take over here?" The sheriff asked.

"Sure thing," Deputy Jones responded as the sheriff headed towards Anna and Beth to see what all the fuss was about.

"Sheriff, we're so sorry to interrupt," Anna continued, "but we know who did it."

Beth chimed in, "We know who has been starting the fires." She said in a breathy voice.

The sheriff pulled the two women aside. "I've got bad news for you, ladies. Sam didn't even have his truck the day that Eli saw it. It was here in the shop, overnight, waiting for an oil change."

Anna and Beth nodded. "We know it wasn't Sam," Anna whispered, but before they could say anything else, the deputy called out to the sheriff.

"Sheriff, I think you're gonna want to see this," he was waving his arm, motioning him over.

"Ok," the sheriff said, "just hold on and stay right here. Don't go anywhere. I'll be right back."

Anna and Beth nodded. They strained to hear what was being said, but they were too far away.

"Anna!" Beth whispered and pulled her sister close, "Look!"

Out across the empty lot, Anna and Beth could see Ryan standing on the back patio of the Amish Inn. Clearly, Hank had not finished putting up his fence just yet, and the sisters could see Ryan standing there, hands on her hips, watching as Anna and Beth huddled together, just a few feet away from where the sheriff and deputy were questioning Wyatt.

Beth looked back to where the sheriff and deputy were standing with Wyatt and watched as Wyatt handed a folded white piece of paper to the sheriff. Wyatt looked up, and when he saw Ryan standing on the back patio, he lifted his arm and pointed at her. Both the sheriff and the deputy turned their heads in her direction. Beth and Anna looked that way, as well, and they all watched as Ryan took off running, disappearing around the other side of the inn.

The sheriff yelled "Ryan! Stop!" and he and the deputy quickly pursued her on foot, sprinting past Anna and Beth.

The sisters ran to their horse and buggy and Beth jumped in. She looked over at Anna who remained standing on the ground. "Come on, Anna! We can stop her!" Beth said firmly. She knew Anna was scared, but she didn't want Ryan to get away.

"Beth, we are not going to be able to stop her. We are not police officers. And the last time I was riding high-speed with you in a buggy, we almost died." Anna said. "I'm staying out of this and leaving it to the police," she said.

"Anna, please get in," Beth pleaded with her sister. "I promise I'll be careful! We can't let Ryan get away or we'll always worry about the next fire!" She begged Anna, but Anna took a step back. "I'm sorry, Beth, I promised Eli."

"Anna," Beth said more calmly now. "We've come so far. Please come with me. I need you. And Little Valley needs you."

Anna sighed and climbed into the buggy slowly, without saying a word. She grabbed a hold of the handle on her right with both hands.

Beth looked at her and smiled, *"Denki, Schwester."* She signaled for her horse to gallop, and he ran. The breeching held secure, and the buggy held tight as Beth and Anna caught up to the sheriff and deputy in no time. They could see Ryan still running about half a mile ahead.

Beth yelled, "Whoa!" to her horse and the horse came to a stop. Beth jumped out and yelled for Anna to do the same. Beth didn't have to tell Anna twice. She was eager to get out of the buggy. She moved fast and was by Beth's side in an instant.

Beth gave the reins to the sheriff. The deputy climbed into where Anna was sitting, and Beth gave the signal to her horse to start running. They took off in Ryan's direction as the sisters stood, arm in arm, safe and sound, watching Ryan being handcuffed only minutes later. The sisters remained silent, both overcome by emotion. It was finally over.

Chapter Twenty-Three

Anna and Beth sat outside on Beth's front porch enjoying the cool breeze and warm sunshine that Little Valley weather offered on a Spring afternoon. They had spent the morning baking with Eva, preparing for the farmers' market the next day. The day before, the women rested between visits from their fellow Amish family and friends. Word of Ryan's arrest had spread, and the sisters were showered with wonderful gifts of delicious food, flowers, and kind words and sweet sentiments. The entire community felt a sense of relief knowing that the person responsible for all the recent fires was sitting behind bars, and once again, they had Anna and Beth to thank for their help.

"Those snowdrop bulbs really did turn out nicely this year, didn't they?" Anna asked, admiring their beauty. "I wasn't sure when you planted them if they were going to disappoint you like the tulips the year before."

"Oh, right. Those silly tulips. I think I needed better soil for those. Maybe I'll try those again next year," Beth said. She loved the way the phrase "next year" sounded. She smiled and let out a quiet happy sigh.

The sheriff's car pulled up in front of Beth and Anna's homes. Sherriff Streen and Deputy Jones stepped out of the car, both greeting Anna and Beth with cheerful faces. Anna and Beth stood up and waved hello. They were excited to see the men and couldn't wait to hear more details about the arrest.

"*Gute daag,*" the sheriff said, his accent a little off. He laughed and asked, "Did I say that right?"

"You were close enough," Anna said.

Beth said, "Not bad at all for an *Englisher!*" They all laughed.

"Come on in," said Anna. "Can I get you some tea or anything?"

"No, thank you, and don't get up," Mark said. "It's a beautiful day. Let's just sit outside and chat."

Christopher spoke up, "I agree! This weather is absolutely perfect!"

"That sounds good to me, too," Beth said, nodding and sitting back down on the swing, patting the seat next to her for Anna to join her. Anna sat and the sisters leaned back. They began to move the swing slowly back and forth, relaxing with the movement. The men each took a seat on the cushioned tall Adirondack chairs.

"This is way too comfortable," Christopher joked. "Am I seriously getting paid to sit outside on this beautiful day with you fine folks in these amazing chairs?" He chuckled.

"This is the good life, for sure," Mark agreed. Then, as if it were an afterthought, "Something tells me Noah Troyer made these chairs, by the way, Christopher, if you're looking for some porch furniture for that new house of yours."

"Ah, good to know. Good to know," Christopher nodded.

"So, tell us! We're so eager to hear about the arrest! We want to hear all about it!" Beth had been so patient, waiting to hear more about what happened.

"Oh, right. We're here on police business," Mark teased. "Well, before I get into it, I have to ask how you two knew that Ryan was the criminal starting all the fires. Was it something her mother said?"

"Well, kind of," Anna responded. "We found a sketch pad in the very back of the far left cabinet in the Amish Inn. As you probably know by now, Ryan was an artist well before she was a chef. She only went to culinary school because she couldn't support herself with her art."

Beth interrupted, "Which is actually surprising when you see her drawings. She is quite good."

"It's true," said Anna.

Beth continued the story where Anna left off. "The sketch pad showed her designs to renovate and redesign the Little Valley Pub. She dreamed of making it a five-star restaurant. She had picked out a name, she drew what the interior would look like, that sort of thing."

Beth paused and Anna spoke up, "Ryan's mother, Shannon, had mentioned that there was a wedge in their relationship, that Ryan always thought Shannon favored Sam. Shannon believes Sam is a smart businessman, but we got the impression that she had little of the same faith in her daughter, unfortunately."

As if they were taking turns, Beth spoke up next, "But what really convinced us was the question mark at the bottom of the drawing. It was the same intricate question mark that she had written on the notes."

"And the paper was the same type of paper, too. You know, it was a little bit heavier weight than normal," Anna chimed in. Both sisters were leaning forward now, reliving the exhilaration of finding the sketch pad.

The sheriff said, "That's really incredible that you found the sketch pad. We are going to go confiscate that just as soon as we leave here to make sure that we have enough circumstantial evidence to prosecute Ryan. And, we'll search Ryan's home to see if we can find some more of her writing to compare with the notes." Christopher nodded.

The sheriff spoke again, "So that's what you were trying to tell me in the Nichols Garage. I see now."

"*Ja*, that was what we were trying to tell you before she took off running," Anna said.

"But what did you find out about Sam's truck?" Beth asked. "We still haven't closed that loop in our heads, and can't figure that one out."

Christopher interjected, looking at Mark. "Shall I tell?" He asked, leaning forward, one elbow on his knee.

"Be my guest," said Mark, smiling.

"So, as it turned out, Sam had actually turned his truck into the Nichols Garage for an oil change the day before the fire was set on your barn, Mrs. Miller. Wyatt Nichols had been too busy to get to it before he closed that day, so he parked it around back to take care of first thing in the morning. Coincidentally, there was a baseball game on that afternoon when Ryan came into his shop just after hours. She explained who she was, Sam's sister, that she worked next door, and Sam had asked her to grab something out of his trunk."

"Distracted by the game, Wyatt handed over the keys to Ryan and she never brought them back." Christopher continued, the sisters listening attentively like children being told a story around a bonfire. He continued, "Wyatt didn't even think about it until the next day when he opened shop and he realized he didn't have Sam's keys. He walked around back and Sam's truck was parked where he had left it, so he opened the driver side door, suspicious that Ryan must have just left the keys inside."

"Sure enough," Christopher explained, "Wyatt found the keys, but he also found a strange note on the ground right by the truck, as well. The note was a folded up piece of heavier than normal paper - now we know that to be sketch pad paper," he smiled. "He picked up the note and thought it must've fallen out of the truck and onto the ground, but he shoved it in his pocket and meant to ask Sam about it when he picked up the truck."

"Ah! She was going to leave that note on your door, Anna, before Eli saw her and she had to run," Beth was putting the pieces together in her head.

"Just out of curiosity, what did the note say?" Anna asked, her forehead wrinkled and her head cocked just off center.

Christopher looked at Mark who waved his hand as if to signal that he could continue with the story, "The last note read one simple sentence: All bets are off." Christopher paused.

"Hmmm," Beth thought out loud. "I don't understand the meanings of the notes."

Mark spoke up, "Yeah, we were confused about that, too, until Ryan started saying things like: 'It wasn't me, it was Sam Graber. Read the notes?' Then, we put two and two together and realized that since Sam wasn't successfully framed for the first fire, she had to turn up the heat - no pun intended," he chuckled, "and start to write the notes to put more suspicion on him."

The sisters both nodded. It was all becoming clear now.

"So, the whole thing wasn't even about us. Our community had nothing to do with it," Beth said, looking at Anna.

Anna nodded and said, "Ja, the crimes were driven by jealousy."

Christopher added, "And jealousy of Sam Graber, of all people, too." He shook his head.

Mark said, "In my line of work, I've noted that jealousy hardly ever works on its own. In most cases, jealousy is a cousin of greed, and I think that's what was happening here, too. It sounds to me like we're going to find out that maybe Sam doesn't own the pub... or maybe he doesn't own it yet. It wouldn't surprise me if Shannon Graber holds the deed to that place and only had intentions of leaving it to Sam, not Ryan."

"Wow," said Beth. Anna shook her head.

"And did you two hear about how we went with Jacob Schwartz and Bishop Packer to meet with Sam yesterday afternoon?" Christopher asked.

Beth gasped. "No, we didn't hear about that," she said, instinctively reaching for her sister's hand.

"Well, it's the perfect ending to the story, actually," Mark said. "I guess Jacob was able to raise the money he owed Sam with all the work he has been able to deliver lately, and he paid his debt in full. Sam agreed to put everything behind him and consider it water under the bridge."

Christopher nodded and smiled, "They shook hands and everything."

The sisters looked at each other, broad smiles spread across their faces. They shared the same thoughts without saying a word. They both knew how hard the community had been working to help Jacob's business get back on track.

Beth muttered another favorite Amish proverb, "Many hands make light work."

Mark grinned, "Well, I would say that's gotta be the perfect proverb for all of this."

Chapter Twenty-Four

---·◦·---

Tulip Park was buzzing with people of all ages, gathered to attend another wonderful farmers' market weekend in Little Valley. This weekend's farmers' market was organized with a Spring seasonal theme, and the local vendors seemed excited to take the lead on offering goods that represented the season. Booths were set up around the perimeter of the park, offering an array of things like rosewater infused handmade soaps and lotions, strawberry ice cream, cherry blossom scented candles, and of course, Spring inspired Amish baked goods.

Anna, Beth and Eva kept busy welcoming family, friends and new customers as they stopped by to purchase treats or to just say hello. Their table was drawing a lot of attention with a white lace table runner positioned over the center of a bright yellow tablecloth. A silver tray of sugar cookies with strawberry frosting and another tray of stained-glass cookies were on one side of the table, and a tiered display of cupcakes with beautifully piped butter-cream frosting made to look like flowers was on the other. A pile of lavender paper napkins sat neatly in the center, a small smooth stone placed on top to keep them from blowing away in the light breeze.

"Wow! This is quite the turnout!" Eva said with excitement as she reached down to grab a box of cookies. The tray of sugar cookies was almost empty, and she took the free second to restock it.

Beth smiled, "*Ja*, it is another beautiful day in Little Valley!" The sisters waved to Jessica McLean as she approached the table.

"Well, hi there! Y'all are sure busy! Ooohh! Your cookies look delicious! I'm not at all surprised!" She said, rubbing her hands together.

"The only surprise here is that you still have cookies left! Look at those beauties!" Matthew Beiler said, appearing out of nowhere.

Jessica's face beamed at the sight of Matthew. "Hi, there, Matthew! Good to see you!"

"Hi, Jessica! I saw you earlier. I was wondering if you were going to come say hello." He teased.

"I just hadn't made it over to see your beautiful flowers yet, but I had definitely planned on it," she smiled and pushed a strand of curly hair out of her face.

He looked almost mesmerized by her movement. Beth watched the scene in front of her and elbowed Anna. Matthew cleared his throat and shook his head lightly as if he were snapping out of a trance. He turned to Anna and Beth and held out a small vase of tulips to Anna. "I brought this to add to your table," he smiled.

"*Denki*, Matthew! They are lovely," Anna said. Beth set the vase on the table, grinning from ear to ear, and arranged the flowers until they formed a perfectly symmetrical arrangement.

"They're perfect!" Beth said, "*Denki*, Matthew! How are things going over there?" She nodded in the direction of his flower booth across the park. Logan Clark was manning the booth.

"Very *gut*!" Matthew said, "And I should probably get back over there and relieve Logan. He has been working very hard helping out at the shop these past few days. I will see you two at dinner tomorrow night." He nodded to the sisters, and then to Jessica, he touched the tip of his hat and said, "I'll see you later this afternoon at the diner?"

"I hope so," Jessica said, smiling with closed lips, her cheeks turning light pink.

Beth hated to do it, but she interrupted. "Before you leave, I want to introduce the both of you to our cousin, Eva Zook," Beth said, gently pulling Eva over to say hello.

"Eva, this is Jessica McLean. She owns Heaven's Diner in town, and this is Matthew Beiler. Matthew owns the flower shop across the street from the diner," Beth said.

She turned to stand next to Eva, facing Jessica and Matthew, "Eva is our second cousin. She traveled here from Worthton. She is a very talented baker and helped us make our selection of cookies today."

"Oh, very nice to meet you, Eva! How are you liking Little Valley?" Jessica asked.

Eva responded, "I like it very much, thank you! I love the name of your diner. I look forward to eating there soon."

Matthew greeted Eva next, welcoming her to town, then politely said, "I should run. I will see you tomorrow night, as well, then!"

"*Ja*, I will be there," Eva responded cheerily.

"Have a *gut* day," Matthew said with a wave before he walked back across the park.

As Eva and Jessica continued to chat about Eva's travels, baking, and life in Little Valley, Deputy Jones approached with two cute little blonde-haired boys in tow. "Good afternoon, Anna and Beth!" He said, holding on to his sons' hands tightly.

"*Hallo*, Christopher!" The sisters welcomed him with a warm smile. "Who do we have here?" Anna asked, sharing a friendly smile with the children.

"Billy and Stephen, say hello to Mrs. Miller and Mrs. Troyer, and you can pick out one cookie each," Christopher said, bent slightly at the waist.

"They look so much like you," Beth said, "Please help yourself. Do we get to meet your wife today?"

"Ah, yes, she is around here somewhere," Christopher said, looking around, just as a woman with short blonde hair and warm brown eyes walked up and slipped her hand into one of the boy's hands.

"Hi! I'm Suzanne. Christopher has told me so much about you two! It's really great to meet you!" She said, smiling.

"It's so nice to meet you, too," Anna said. "We are big fans of your husband."

Sheriff Mark Streen walked up next, "Well, fancy meeting the Jones family here! And hello, Beth and Anna! I'm glad you are getting to meet everyone! Aren't these boys just the cutest?"

"*Hallo*, Sheriff! Great to see you today! Please, help yourself to a cookie," Beth said.

"Oh, I can't. I've been eating too many cookies lately," he laughed, patting his stomach.

"Nonsense. There is no such thing as too many cookies," Anna said, chuckling.

"It's true, Sheriff," Jessica chimed in before extending a handshake and introduction to Suzanne Jones.

Beth said, "Oh, Sheriff Streen, meet Eva Zook. She's our cousin from Worthton. She's here in Little Valley learning some baking techniques from me and Anna, but she's opening a bakery on the corner of First Avenue and Jefferson here in a few weeks." She continued introducing Eva to the deputy and his family, as well.

"Well, congratulations, Eva, and welcome to town!" said the sheriff. "I'll pass the word about your new bakery."

"What?! I didn't know about that," Jessica exclaimed! "That's so exciting! We'll definitely have to talk more. You'll be right around the corner from my diner! Let me know if you need help with anything."

"Thank you so much," Eva said graciously.

The day continued with similar wonderful visits from Anna and Beth's children and grandchildren and from new friends and old. The women's cookie and cupcake supply ran dry just before the market came to a close. Eli and Noah jumped in to help break down the booth, pack up and load the buggy to head home.

After an easy dinner of leftovers, Beth headed over to Anna's house to say goodnight and spend a few minutes recapping the day. She knocked softly on the back door, entering quietly. She knew Eli would already be in bed. He woke early each morning to start his day on the farm which meant he was also typically the first to turn in for the night.

Anna was sitting in her rocking chair, her crochet needles in hand, a blanket draped across her lap. She called softly for Beth to come in.

"*Hallo, Schwester*," Beth whispered as she tiptoed across the kitchen floor into the living room.

Anna chuckled, "You know you don't have to be that quiet."

Beth grinned and settled onto the couch next to Anna's chair. "I can't believe you haven't finished that blanket yet. It feels like you've been working on it for months," she teased.

"I'm taking my time," Anna said with a small smile. Her hands continued to move the needles methodically.

Beth stretched her arms above her head before relaxing them again, leaning back on the couch. "It was a good day, huh?" She asked.

"*Ja*, it was, indeed," Anna responded. "I was just thinking about how lucky we are to live in such a *wunderbaar* town, surrounded by so many loving friends and family." Anna paused briefly before continuing, "With all that this town has been through, it's the people that truly are the saving grace."

Beth grinned. It made her so happy to hear her sister say those words.

———◇———

Eva soon realizes just how much she needs Anna and Beth's sleuthing skills when she becomes the prime murder suspect in the next story in the Amish Lantern Mystery Series. It almost feels like deja vu to the sisters as they are once again faced with clearing their family's name, but things become even more complicated than ever before since the murder weapon has Eva's prints all over it.

Good Intentions is the fourth (and next!) book in the Amish Lantern Mystery Series. Visit my website at **marybbarbee.com** to grab your copy!

Is your mouth watering after reading all about those delicious Amish treats? Visit

marybbarbee.com/ALMS-cookbook to get instant access to *The Amish Lantern Mystery Series Cookbook*. You'll find Anna and Beth's Dark Chocolate Pie and Strawberry Cream Cheese Danish recipes... and so much more, including a few extra flavorful recipes that are introduced later in the Amish Lantern Mystery Series.

Acknowledgments

Gratitude is a big part of the Amish culture, and it's an important part of my life, too. This book simply wouldn't be ready on time, or maybe near as enjoyable, if it weren't for a few very important people. And so, I want/need to take the time to send my love here.

I am dedicating this book to Yoko. She was my rescue pup, and I had the great pleasure of sharing my life with her for over seven wonderful years. She was my little writing buddy, snuggled up next to me while I wrote into the late hours of the night. Life looks different now, but she's forever with me in my heart. I am so grateful for the lessons of love and dedication that she taught me.

Thank you, again, to all my friends, my family, and my readers – I'm not sure there's much difference between those three! Your support is unwavering, and I continue to be overwhelmed with gratitude as I receive your beautiful compliments.

Thank you, thank you, thank you to my mother, Molly Misko, my dear friend, Jenny Raith, and my sweet sister, Julie Rietze. Your unwavering dedication to read, review and suggest edits along the way of each of my books' journey is so amazing. Your insight, your support, and your love shine through in every single comment you leave, and in every conversation we have. I can't thank you enough for everything you do.

As the Amish say beautifully, *Denki*. I am forever grateful.

A Note From the Author

---◆◆◆---

Thank you for reading *Saving Grace*. I wrote this book a little bit differently than any other book in the past – I started with the title.

The title of this book actually came to me during the time when I was still writing *Secrets in Little Valley*. I was playing a game of tennis with my mother one early morning, and she was winning. She served a double fault, and I thought to myself, *well, that was my saving grace*. I had this strange reaction to the phrase "saving grace" in my head, like *where did that come from?* It definitely wasn't a phrase I use often, but I immediately knew that was going to be the name of my next book.

Per usual, when I have an idea like that, I can't let it go. So, I wrapped up *Secrets in Little Valley* and found myself super excited to get started on *Saving Grace*. As I started writing, though, I ran into writers' block after writers' block. I think the biggest struggle was due to the coincidence that Grace was Ruby's best friend in *Secrets in Little Valley*. I didn't want her to experience any danger since Ruby was the victim in the previous book. I knew I needed to have another twist.

I had also decided that I wanted to veer away from murder for this book. I know it's fiction, and this is a cozy mystery and all, but I just wasn't sure about there being a murder in the charming, small town of Little Valley every few months or so. I wanted to change things up a bit.

I loved introducing new characters in Saving Grace, and there turned out to be quite a lot of opportunity to do so. And, as always, I enjoyed developing the sisters' characters, as well. And finally, my editor, and friend, insisted that I include recipes again, so cheers to Jenny Raith for pushing that to be a tradition.

If you're on the edge of your seat, wanting to read more about the wonderful people of Little Valley, please visit my website at marybbarbee.com to sign up for my new release email list.

Thank you again for choosing *Saving Grace* to add to your book selection. If you enjoyed it, please consider leaving a review on Goodreads or Bookbub – or simply by recommending it to a friend!

With so much gratitude,

Mary B. Barbee

About the Author

---◆○◆---

Mary B. Barbee is the author of the *Amish Lantern Mystery Series*. As an avid fan of all mystery and suspense in print, on television and in film, Mary B. believes the best mystery is one where the suspect changes throughout the story, keeping the audience guessing. She enjoys providing an exciting escape for a few hours with stories her readers can't put down - and always with a surprise ending.

When not writing, Mary B. is either playing a couple sets of tennis or a strategy board game with her two witty daughters and her kindly competitive mother. The four of them share a home in the Inland Northwest in the beautiful town of Spokane, Washington with their really cute - but sometimes naughty - chihuahua.

Mary B. loves to hear from her readers. Connect at:
marybbarbee@gmail.com
www.facebook/marybbarbee
Instagram @marybbarbee
www.marybbarbee.com

More Books to Read By Mary B. Barbee

THE AMISH LANTERN MYSTERY SERIES

Thick As Thieves – Book 1

Robberies are running rampant in Little Valley, and the quiet small-town lives of the Amish community are suddenly thrown into chaos.

Secrets in Little Valley – Book 2

With the bishop's daughter suddenly missing and a new sheriff in town, Anna and Beth find themselves roped into solving another mystery in their small town.

Saving Grace – Book 3

The Amish community in Little Valley is facing big changes, and big threats, with tourism booming. It becomes clear that some of the new businesses want control of the market, and it looks like they are willing to go to great lengths to get it.

Good Intentions – Book 4

Hazel Thompson is found dead in Little Valley's now-famous Amish Inn, and there's a long list of suspects with plenty of motive.

A Blessing in Disguise – Book 5

Jessica McLean opens shop to find a man has been left for dead on the floor of her diner. Could the crime could be related to Jessica's new relationship with their beloved Matthew Beiler?

Christmas Chaos in Little Valley - Book 6

Beth finds out that the Little Valley library is shutting its doors due to a lack of funding and very disturbing anonymous threats.

——◦——

THE ABIGAIL BAKER MYSTERY SERIES
Blind Faith – Prequel
Abigail's excitement for her new home is replaced by doom and gloom when she finds out that an unexplained murder has rocked the residents of her new town. And not unusual to her, it's the Amish community that is suspect number one.

**Grab your free e-copy of Blind Faith at:
marybbarbee.com/blindfaith**

Where Fear Ends – Book 1
A town councilman is found dead by the side of the road in the Amish community of Abigail Baker's new hometown.

A Multitude of Sins – Book 2

When secret notes containing serious threats are unveiled, Abigail wonders if the latest victim could have been hiding a multitude of sins.

A Wing and a Prayer – Book 3 ~ COMING SOON!

THE PUPCAKE MYSTERY SERIES
Cupcakes and Corruption – Prequel
Battling empty-nest syndrome, Eliza finds solace in the company of her adorable chihuahua, Pupcake, and her dreams of opening a quaint coffee shop. Little does she know that her talent for baking and nurturing also extends to amateur sleuthing.

Grab your free e-copy of Cupcakes and Corruption at:
marybbarbee.com/pupcakeprequel

Sweet Suspicion – Book 1
The charming town of Copeland is buzzing with excitement as Eliza and her adorable chihuahua, Pupcake, open their new coffee shop. But when a body is discovered on

the premises, the duo must put down their baking tools and pick up their detective hats.

Confections and Clues – Book 2 – Coming Valentine's Day 2025

Eliza and Pupcake's lakeside getaway takes a dark turn when they stumble upon a body. With a secretive small town and a case no one wants solved, Eliza's sweet retreat quickly turns into another mystery. Can she and Pupcake crack the case before the killer's trail goes cold?

Recipe for Reckoning – Book 3 ~ COMING SOON!

Find excerpts, purchase links and more at
www.marybbarbee.com